KHORNDAHGH

THE

BARBARIAN

Tome III: Pretty Pixie

By John Cop

Cover Art by licarto

ISBN: 979-8-9892590-5-2

Any reference to historical events, real people, or real places are used fictitiously. Names, characters, and places are products of the author's imagination.

First printing edition 2025

Published by Super Awesome Stories

Email: superawesomestories@superawesomestories.com

Website: superawesomestories.com

Table of Contents

Chapter 1: Pretty Pixie

Little Cleo stood in a post-apocalyptic forest, brushing Pretty Pixie's hair with a bristle brush. Little Cleo was Cleopatra when she was a little girl, dressed in a stylish boy scout uniform with short shorts and hiking boots. She was standing face to face with her identical twin sister, as if she were looking into a mirror. Little Cleo smiled and said, "Pretty Pixie, you're so pretty!"

Pretty Pixie was Pixie when she was a little girl. She wore a pink and white puffed-sleeve dress with a pinafore and shiny black ankle-strap shoes. Pretty Pixie pointed behind Little Cleo and said, "Rabbit."

Little Cleo turned to see a white rabbit not far away, looking directly at them. She yelled, "Let's get it!" The white rabbit sprang away, Little Cleo dashing after it.

Pretty Pixie gave chase, but she was not as athletic as Little Cleo, and did not have the benefit of hiking boots. Falling behind, she turned on the boosters before tripping and falling flat on her face.

Pretty Pixie tried to cry but found that she couldn't, and instead frowned. She looked up, but didn't see her sister. "Cleo?" Pretty Pixie stood up, brushing off leaves and dirt. Her dress wasn't so pretty now. She shouted for her sister, "Cleo!"

Pretty Pixie looked all around, but didn't see Little Cleo. She did see the white rabbit. The leporidae sat in a small white chair, perched over a small white table, munching baby carrots from a small white plate. Another small white chair sat opposite the white rabbit, its place at the table set with a little chocolate cake on a small white plate. There was no little fork. A note propped up by the cake read, 'DONT EAT ME'.

Pretty Pixie took a seat very properly at the table and picked up the note, then clumsily dropped it. After picking the note back up, she blankly stared at it. It didn't matter that the note was now upside down as she couldn't read it anyway.

Pretty Pixie tossed the note aside and dug into the chocolate cake with her hands. She gobbled down the cake, her pretty face getting chocolate all over it.

The little chocolate cake was so delicious that Pretty Pixie wished it were big. "Big," she said. And just like that, her wish was granted. What was left of the little cake started growing in size, first to a normal size cake, then to the size of a big cake, then to the size of two big cakes! Pretty Pixie smiled delightfully.

The table was also growing big, as were the chairs and the plates and the white rabbit and the post-apocalyptic forest and everything in the world, except for Pretty Pixie. Everything became so big that Pretty Pixie couldn't reach the gigantic little cake. She reached and reached but was getting further and further away from the ever-growing table. She tried crying but everything continued to grow and grow.

In the distance, Pretty Pixie could see a gigantic Little Cleo running towards her in slow motion. Had she sharper eyes, Pretty Pixie would have also spotted an elderly camouflaged faerie with a long gray beard entangling some twigs and leaves, his green and brown robes blending into the foliage.

Gigantic Little Cleo continued to run through the gigantic forest in slow motion. With a deep, unnatural-sounding voice, like a higher-pitched voice slowed down, gigantic Little Cleo shouted, "Piiixxxiiieee!"

The table and the cake and the chairs and the plates and the carrots and the white rabbit all exploded into faerie dust, dropping Pretty Pixie towards the ground. A post-apocalyptic tiger lily caught her before depositing her ungently to the ground, further dirtying her. Still lying on the ground, Pretty Pixie yelled, "Cleo!"

Gigantic Little Cleo was still running towards

Pretty Pixie, but didn't see her tiny form in the grass, nor did she hear her, even though Pretty Pixie continued to shout, "Cleo!" again and again. Gigantic Little Cleo's gigantic hiking boot came down on top of Pretty Pixie, but the tiny girl rolled away from the slow-motion step in the knick of time, further dirtying her dress. "Cleo!" she yelled again.

Gigantic Little Cleo couldn't hear her tiny sister and ran right past her in slow motion, still shouting, "Piiixxxiiieee!" And away she went, slowly running through the forest.

Pretty Pixie's pink dress was by now very dirty. Her hair was all mussed up, and her face and hands were smeared with chocolate frosting. She stood up and weakly cried out, "cleo?" After looking around, she found herself all alone and began crying. That's when she saw the faeries.

At first, a lone faerie girl stepped out of hiding. Her hair was blue and she wore blue faerie garb. Her faerie wings, like that of a dragonfly, flapped slowly with nervous agitation.

Her name was Adelina, and she was a smart and confident faerie. Her propensity to speak her mind had gotten her in trouble on more than one occasion, but she had a good heart and was a natural leader. Adelina spoke, but not to Pretty Pixie, "I told you we should have used an apostrophe."

A male faerie stepped out of hiding. He wore green, leafy garb and atop his head sat a green, feathered bycocket cap. His name was Chepi, and he was a bit of a fanatic when it came to protecting the faerie folk, no matter the cost. His faerie wings flapped with frustration as he responded to Adelina, "Faeries dont use apostrophes."

Another faerie girl, this one adorned in a purple faerie dress, stepped out of hiding. Her beautiful hair was long and wavy-blonde. Her name was Dorielle, and she loved all that was beautiful in the world, including herself. Her faerie wings flapped elegantly, with slow grace. "What do we do with it?" she asked, referring to

Pretty Pixie.

The faeries looked over Pretty Pixie. The now faerie-sized girl beamed with joy at seeing real faeries, and giggled with delight.

Chepi answered Dorielle's query, "We kill it."

"Faeries dont kill!" protested Adelina, her faerie wings flapping anxiously.

"Not directly," explained Chepi.

"Were not killing it," decided Dorielle.

"Then whatta we do?" asked Chepi, "Shes seen us."

Adelina answered, "Pretty Pixie has seen us before. Shes never told. Isnt that right, Pretty Pixie?"

Pretty Pixie nodded, still smiling delightfully.

Dorielle could see Pretty Pixie's beauty beneath the dirt and chocolate frosting, and wanted to help her. "Who made her small?" she asked, twirling her long blonde faerie hair with her faerie finger.

"Another tribe," said Adelina.

"It was Xixer, I bet." suggested Chepi.

"Why would Xixer do it?" asked Adelina.

Chepi explained, "He wants to be Chief."

"That doesnt make sense," said Adelina.

Chepi further explained, "He could blame it on Vicente."

"So whatta we do?" asked Dorielle.

"We take her back," concluded Adelina.

"Back where?" asked Chepi.

"To Faerietown," answered Adelina.

Chepi was unnerved, "Are you crazy?"

Adelina insisted, "We cant leave her here like this. She doesnt have wings. Shell get eaten."

Chepi smirked. "Like I said, indirectly."

"Were not leaving her to get eaten," protested Adelina.

"What then?" asked Dorielle.

"Faerietown," answered Adelina.

"Faerietown," concurred Dorielle.

Chepi dissented, "I just want to state for the record, I think this is a terrible idea, and we should kill it."

"Noted," said Adelina. "Cmon, Pretty Pixie.

Were goin to Faerietown!" Pretty Pixie giggled with joy.

The faeries tramped through the post-apocalyptic forest with Pretty Pixie in tow. Chepi would normally lead, but his reluctance with the mission kept him guarding the rear. Along the journey, the faeries lifted Pretty Pixie over a rivulet of water that to them was like a river. After crossing the stream, the faerie girls smiled and laughed with Pretty Pixie all the way to Faerietown. Chepi was not laughing, and carried with him a sense of doom as they neared the faerie haven.

Upon finally reaching Faerietown, Pretty Pixie looked around in awe. There were faerie houses blending in with the vegetation. There were also faerie fountains, faerie hammocks, faerie waterfalls, and faeries everywhere doing faerie things. Set upon a small table in the middle of town was all manner of sweet treats, including little cakes.

"Are you hungry, Pretty Pixie?" asked

Dorielle.

Pretty Pixie smiled and ran to the table. She immediately began stuffing her face with the sweet treats. Adelina, Dorielle, and Chepi walked up as the Faerietown faeries began to gather around.

"You know the law!" shouted Xixer. Xixer was an elderly faerie with a long white beard. He would have become tribal chieftain many solstices ago if not for Vicente, who had managed to stay alive long beyond his expiration date. Given Vicente's rapidly decreasing mental acuity and strange outbursts, Xixer thought it only wise to remove Vicente to a faerie sanitarium, and that he, Xixer, be placed in power. But Vicente refused, and that was that.

Chepi answered Xixer, "Not my call. I wanted to leave her."

Adelina protested, "She would have been eaten by an animal!"

"And look how pretty Pretty Pixie is," added Dorielle.

Pretty Pixie continued to stuff her face with sweet treats.

Xixer exclaimed, "You will be punished, and the invader fed to carrion fowl! She wont be so pretty then."

An elderly hand came down on Xixer's shoulder, the hand of Vicente, Chief of the White Rabbit faerie tribe. Xixer receded as Vicente stepped forward. "There will be no punishment," said the eldest of the faeries, whose gray beard entangled some twigs and leaves. Vicente was very very old, increasingly confused and prone to bouts of nonsense. Today, however, his wits were sharp, even if his sanity was still in question.

"You know the law!" accused Xixer.

"I am the law," countered Vicente. This shut up Xixer, who further receded into the gathered faerie crowd.

"Whatta we do with her then?" asked Chepi.

Vincente proclaimed, "We will take her in and protect her. She will be one of the tribe."

"Thats never been done," warned Chepi.

Adelina rebuffed, "Weve had faerie friends among the big folk before."

"Theyve never been brought home," said Chepi.

Dorielle did a hair flip to adjust her flowing blonde locks, and responded, "This is Pretty Pixie's home now."

Pretty Pixie was still stuffing her face with the sweet treats, some of it winding up on her face and dress.

Chepi warned, "We cant always protect her. Its only a matter of time before–"

"We will teach her faerie magic," said Vicente. "If she is to be one of us, then she must be one of us."

"Are you sure thats a good idea?" asked Chepi, highly skeptical of the plan.

Vicente was sure. "Pretty Pixie has a pure heart. She will make an excellent faerie. So it is said, so it shall be done."

The gathered faeries smiled at Pretty Pixie, who grinned like the Cheshire Cat.

And so Pretty Pixie lived with the faeries and learned faerie magic. It was clear to the other faeries that she was not good at it, but Pretty Pixie seemed happy with the results, however unexpected they were.

Just as everything seemed to be going swimmingly, Pretty Pixie started crying. Adelina asked her, "Whats wrong, Pretty Pixie?"

Pretty Pixie remembered, "Cleo!"

Chapter 2: The Supercar

Cleopatra sat in the driver seat of the parked 1957 Mercedes-Benz 300 SL Roadster open convertible. The supercar's 3.14 liter zero-point energy supercharged mercury centrifuge engine was silent. Cleopatra's blue Versace dress was torn and dirtied by battle and nursing. The gigantic fiery morning sun, appearing so due to the Multapocalyptic Atmospheric Lensing Effect, rose above the horizon of the barren post-apocalyptic Arizona desert.

The gorilla, Etty, sat in the passenger seat. Cleopatra tried to work the gear shifter, but Etty's arm was in the way. The gorilla's shouldered satchel wasn't helping either. The stack of golden halos that Cleopatra had put in between them was even more unhelpful. Etty would have rather been driving. His brain crystals glowed with red light.

Khorndahgh the Barbarian was behind the supercar, his abdomen wrapped up with the ripped off part of Cleopatra's Versace dress. He improperly opened the trunk without pushing the release button, breaking off the lock and bending the hood in the process. Looking inside, he found Marvin's zero-point energy supercharged mercury centrifuge powered flight harness within. The flight harness bore the scars of battle, its robotic arms severed, and the net line cut. Khorndahgh climbed into the trunk and sat atop the flight harness.

Up front, Cleopatra and Etty were involved in a handsy war. "Do you mind?" said Cleopatra, annoyed. Etty scrunched over as much as he was willing. Cleopatra probably had enough room to operate the vehicle, but flared her elbow out to make it seem as though she didn't. "This isn't going to work," she said.

Etty agreed, "Fine, I'll drive."

"You're an animal. You don't know how to

drive," stated Cleopatra.

Etty rebutted, "I do know how to drive. Unlike you, I've actually driven a car. I've also read a manual on it, so I know how it all works."

"This is different," said Cleopatra.

Etty inquired, "Have you ever driven anything?"

"No."

"So I should drive," concluded Etty, rationally.

"You don't even know how z-point energy works."

Etty was deeply stung by this remark, with what happened at the movie theater. He shot back, "Neither do you."

"I've seen Marvin do it. I just need more space." Cleopatra ended her statement staring directly into Etty's simian eyes.

"Well, what do you suggest then?" asked the ape.

Cleopatra looked back at the trunk, then to Etty again.

"You're joking," said Etty, in disbelief.

"It's the only h'way," responded Cleopatra, and not nicely.

Etty sighed, his brain crystals turning blue. He slowly extracted himself from the supercar via the passenger door. After exiting the vehicle, the gorilla grabbed the stack of golden halos from the car and dropped them to the ground. Closing the door, he responded to Cleopatra's disapproving stare, saying, "More space," before moping back to the trunk and staring blankly at Khorndahgh, who stared blankly back.

Cleopatra broke the stare contest, "Khorndahgh, come sit up front."

Etty's brain crystals turned green as Khorndahgh hopped out of the trunk and moved to the passenger door. The barbarian leaped into the passenger seat, forgoing the door. He thought it best to leap, having a poor track record with car doors.

Etty's brain crystals glowed with multicolored lights when he saw Marvin's flight harness in the trunk. The crystals' lights faded out as the gorilla cried, "Bingo!"

Cleopatra wondered out loud, "Why would Marvin have travel bingo? We can go anywhere instantly."

Etty's crystals lit up with blacklight. He began to answer, but stopped, deciding to keep it to himself. Cleopatra was a disappointment to Etty. She was not at all what he expected, and he wanted Pixie back. He rationalized, perhaps correctly, that Cleopatra's mind was not the best mind for use of the flight harness.

Cleopatra smiled at Khorndahgh, now sitting comfortably next to her with a muscled arm resting on the back of her seat. Cleopatra was impressed by the specimen. "You work out?" she asked.

"Every day," replied the barbarian, returning the smile.

"It shows."

The front end of the supercar suddenly rose into the air, a result of the gorilla climbing into the trunk.

"We're flying!" exclaimed Khorndahgh.

"Yeah, but not moving," said Cleopatra, confused.

Etty spoke from behind the hood of the trunk, "Maybe that's how z-point energy works."

"This is not how I remember it," said Cleopatra.

Etty carefully got out of the trunk and put his paws on the back bumper, slowly lowering the front end, mindful not to cause any damage, after which he and Khorndahgh switched places again. Etty was in a much better mood already. His crystals glowed with blacklight as he thought about how to make use of Marvin's flight harness from his upgraded seat.

Cleopatra began the car-starting ritual, "Okay, ready?"

"No," replied Etty.

"You're not ready?"

"Not ready for *your* driving."

Cleopatra was offended. "So girls can't drive?"

"Pixie drove," replied Etty.

"See, girls can drive. What are you afraid of?"

Etty divulged the results of the faerie magician's turn at the wheel, "She almost crashed three times. And that was without petrol."

"I won't crash. Might break a nail," said Cleoptra, winning the argument.

Etty frowned, his brain crystals turning red.

"Okay, ready?" said Cleoptatra, again.

Etty sat in silence.

Cleopatra tried again, "Ready?"

Etty responded, "As ready as I'll ever be."

"You're not doing it right. It's not going to work."

"Not doing what right?"

"I say 'ready?' then you say 'punch it!'"

"I'm pretty sure this machine does not require me to say anything," postulated Etty, correctly.

"Just do it."

Etty sighed.

"Okay, ready?" said Cleopatra, yet again.

Etty executed his task with peak blandness, "punch it."

Cleopatra put the pedal to the metal, but nothing happened. She tried again, still nothing.

"Maybe you should start the engine first," suggested Etty.

"Oh, right." Cleopatra searched for the ignition switch and found it on the dashboard. "I found the keyhole."

Etty informed, "It's called an ignition switch."

"Keyhole makes more sense. Anyway, that's where the key goes." They sat in silence for a moment before Cleoptra spoke again, "Do you have the keys?"

The red glow in Etty's crystals brightened. "Why would *I* have the keys?"

"Never know."

Etty was, by now, very annoyed. "Great. We have a flying car that can go anywhere instantly, but you forgot the keys."

"I didn't forget 'em. Marvin has 'em."

"I'm surprised you didn't pick his pocket."

Cleopatra protested, "I'm not a thief."

"I'll have to take your word for it," said the ape. "So what now?"

"There's gotta be a way."

Etty's brain crystals glowed with blacklight. "There is."

"Okay, what do I do?" asked Cleopatra, hoping the solution didn't involve a gorilla driving her car.

Etty missed the opportunity, instead being honest, "I don't know exactly. There's a switch inside the keyhole that turns, I think."

"How do I open it?"

"With tools, I suppose," said Etty, somewhat disinterested.

Cleopatra glanced at the ruins of Phoenix in the distance. "Know of any hardware stores close by?" Cleopatra was beginning to get hungry, which was something she had not felt in a very long time, having been well-fed in captivity. "Or an Olive Garden?"

Etty ignored the Olive Garden remark, as it

was silly, and he was used to being hungry. "There might be some tools in the limousine," he said, a little mad at himself for not doing a thorough search of the Cadillac.

Cleopatra again looked at the ruins of Phoenix in the distance. "It's a long walk," she said, before turning and staring at Etty.

Etty knew what to do, and walking all the way back to Phoenix was not it. "Khorndahgh!"

Khorndahgh hopped out of the trunk and walked up to Etty. The barbarian and Cleopatra shared a smile.

Etty gave his orders, "Khorndahgh, we need you to go to the limousine. You're looking for tools. First look in the trunk, then check the secret compartment. You can access that by–"

Khorndahgh stared blankly at Etty, interrupting the gorilla's train of thought. His mind cleared, Etty came up with a better idea, "You know what, just bring the limo here."

Khorndhagh nodded to Etty. After another smile with Cleoptra, the barbarian dashed away.

"He must have a lot of girlfriends," said Cleopatra.

"All over the world," admitted Etty.

"Is Pixie–?"

"No," said the ape, not liking the impending question. His crystals glowed in a patchwork of red, pink, and green.

"But he does have girlfriends. So where's all the little Khorndahghs?"

"Checkers," said Etty, his brain crystals now glowing with blacklight.

"What?"

"He plays checkers with them. It's his favorite thing to do after fighting."

"Checkers?" said Cleopatra, incredulous.

"You didn't think it was chess, did you?"

"No, I thought it was something else."

Etty frowned and looked off into the distance through his nerdy repaired eyeglasses, wanting to think about more important things.

"So what happened?" asked Cleopatra.

"He wins, but I think they let him."

Cleopatra clarified, "Not them, you."

"What?" said Etty, snapping his head around.

Cleopatra asked very precisely, "What happened when Etty played Khorndahgh in checkers?"

Etty's crystals turned pink. "How do you know that I did?"

Cleopatra smiled. A short laugh escaped her lips.

Etty stated very formally, "The first rule of checkers is 'you do not talk about Etty v Khorndahgh checkers.'"

"Why?"

"The second rule of checkers is 'you do not talk about Etty v Khorndahgh checkers.'"

Cleopatra was again incredulous. "You lost?"

Etty's brain crystals turned red. "I didn't say I lost."

"So what happened?"

Etty repeated, "The first rule of checkers is—"

"--you don't talk about it...right, I get it." Cleopatra chuckled. "Wish I was there."

"No, you don't," said the gorilla, regretful he had brought it up.

Chapter 3: The Prisoner

Pixie was dressed in a stylish, old-timey prison uniform with black and white stripes that she had conjured up with her faerie magic. She sat on a short bench in a tiny wooden room, bathed in darkness. On the bench next to her sat a rotten apple core and Cleopatra's partly burned and torn copy of Agatha Christie's *Death on the River Nile*. Pixie hung her head and cried softly.

A tiny window in front of Pixie slid open, revealing a criss-cross wooden lattice. Light streamed in from beyond like the rays of the sun. Pixie didn't flinch, and continued sobbing.

Pope spoke from beyond the tiny window, "Say 'forgive me Father for I have sinned.'" Not getting a response, Pope repeated his command, "Say 'forgive me Father for I have sinned.'"

Pixie continued sobbing.

"Say it!" commanded the robot pope.

Nothing.

"You will be punished if you do not obey," stated Pope.

Zilch.

Pope tried biblical love, "Revelations 3:19 'Those who have earned my love I scold and discipline, so be zealous and repent.'"

Zip.

Pope next tried biblical wrath, "Romans 13:4 'I am God's avenger, who carries out God's wrath on the wrongdoer.'"

Nada.

Pope tried wrath again, "Proverbs 11:21 'Be assured, evildoers will not go unpunished.'"

Still nothing.

Pope tried cherry-picking phrases from a biblical passage, "Luke 13:3 'Unless you repent,' 'You will perish.'"

Sobs.

Pope next tried adding clarification to a biblical passage, "Luke 12:48 'If you do not cooperate,' 'you will receive a light beating.'"

Nothing was working, and so Pope gave up, saying, "Galatians 6:7 'God is not mocked.'"

Pixie continued sobbing as the shutter on the tiny window slid closed and a swooshing door was heard on the other side.

Marvin waited outside the confessional in the Sistine Chapel, dressed in a red space-emperor outfit, size XXXL. He was flanked by two rook robots. The Red Vine mark across his face had not faded, and he wore a cast brace on his right wrist, which had been injured by Cleopatra's karate chop. Hammerhead robots were positioned throughout the chapel. After Pope exited the confessional, Marvin said, "That was quick."

"She's a mute," replied Pope.

"She's not a mute. She was yelling 'Cleo' all over the movie theater."

"She isn't like the other one."

"She's a clone. She's exactly like the other one."

"This one's defective," refuted Pope.

Marvin was disappointed in the robot pope. "She's playing you. You don't know how to talk to women, especially not one of her caliber."

Pope motioned to the open confessional door. Marvin passed on the open door and instead opened the door to Pixie's side. He entered and, after brushing aside the rotten apple core, sat next to the girl, closing the door for privacy from Pope's interference.

Seeing Pixie's 'fake' sobs, Marvin took a harsh tone inside the dark confessional, "You can stop playing your games, they won't work on me."

Pixie sobbed some more, her head down.

Marvin exposed the 'con artist,' "Stop the charade, I know all your tricks. You can't win."

Pixie continued sobbing.

Marvin got direct with the girl, "Your clone was the same way until I threatened to have her limbs torn off by robots."

Surprisingly, this threat had no effect, angering Marvin. "Say something!"

Pixie said nothing, unless sobbing was saying something.

Marvin angrily exited the confessional and closed the door. He thought for a moment, then turned to Pope. "She isn't saying anything."

"Told you," said Pope.

"Maybe she's a bad copy."

"Told you," said Pope, again.

Marvin thought for a moment, before conjecturing, "She wasn't programmed. Maybe she's just ignorant, uneducated. Like a child."

"Maybe she has brain damage," said Pope. "Perhaps we should perform a lobotomy."

"I don't think that's necessary," responded Marvin, after thinking about it for a moment.

Pope made another suggestion, "Perhaps you should speak to her as if you were speaking to a child."

Just then, Marvin came up with the solution, "I got it! I'll talk to her like she's a kid."

"Brilliant," said Pope, sarcastically.

Marvin entered the confessional again on

Pixie's side and closed the door. Once inside, he slid open the tiny window, allowing rays of light to stream in through the criss-cross wooden lattice. Turning to Pixie, he said, "Your clone and I had a good relationship. We used to talk all the time. Sometimes I wished she would just shut up, to be honest. But she was my fiancé. Anyway, we were a good match. It's hard to find someone close to my intellect. I tried creating one, but it didn't work out. As the clone of such a fine specimen you can be educated. One day you will be as smart as Cleopatra and—"

"Cleo?" said Pixie, looking up at Marvin with hopeful eyes.

"Cleopatra?" responded Marvin, surprised that Pixie had finally said something.

Pixie smiled.

"You miss Cleopatra," stated Marvin, not needing to ask.

Pixie continued smiling as she nodded, her eyes lighting up.

Marvin reasoned, "Well, she is your clone,

so..."

Pixie turned sad again and hung her head.

"You don't like clones?" asked Marvin.

Pixie remained sad. Marvin became frustrated. This hadn't worked out like he had hoped. He sighed and said, "I wish I had Cleopatra back."

Pixie lit up again. "Cleo?"

"Cleopatra?"

Pixie was still happy.

Marvin began the test, "Clone."

Pixie turned sad.

"Cleopatra."

Pixie turned happy.

"Clone."

Pixie turned sad.

"Cleopatra."

Pixie turned happy.

"Clone."

Pixie turned sad.

Marvin tried to remember the replicant test from the movie *Blade Runner,* "There's a turtle on its back. Whatta ya do?"

This question made Pixie even sadder, and she began crying.

Marvin explained the law to Pixie as gently as he could, "I don't mean to be...mean, but the penalty for building life-like robots is termination...for both." Marvin pinched Pixie's arm, feeling for robotic wiring under her skin. Pixie cried even more. Marvin apologized, "Sorry, I had to be sure. Hang on a second." Marvin exited the confessional and closed the door.

Now back in the Sistine Chapel, Marvin said to Pope, "She's not a robot."

Pope responded, again sarcastically, "I sometimes underestimate your genius."

"She's just dumb."

"I will begin educating her immediately," said Pope.

Immediately was too soon for Marvin. "Before that I'm gonna take her on a date. I don't want her to think I'm a bad guy. I am going to marry her, after all."

Pope proclaimed, "Proverbs 18:22 'He who finds a wife, finds something good, and gains favor from the Lord.'"

"That's what I said."

Pope explained, "That's why I quoted that passage. It wouldn't make any sense to quote a biblical passage unrelated to what you said."

"My point is, it didn't need to be said."

"Didn't it?"

Marvin paused. "I guess you're right. I don't want to end up being the bad guy."

Pope was pleased. "John 10:30 'The Father and I are one.'"

Marvin raised an eyebrow. "By 'I' you mean 'Jesus', right?"

Pope ignored Marvin's question and pulled from his white robes a disordered Rubik's Cube. He suggested, "We should determine her problem-solving skills, so that I may tailor her education."

Just then, Marvin came up with the solution. "I got it! We'll give her an I.Q. test." Marvin snatched the Rubik's Cube out of Pope's robotic hand and opened the confessional door, saying to Pixe, "See this cube? The goal is to make each side a different color. I'll show you. Pope will time me."

Just seconds after Pope said, "Go," Marvin had solved the Rubik's Cube, making every side a different color. Pope announced, "Two point nine-nine seconds. A new record!"

Marvin messed up the colors again and handed the cube to Pixie. "Now you try it. See if you can make a single side all the same color."

Pixie took the Rubik's Cube in hand, thinking it pretty. Just as Pope said, "Go," Pixie touched the cube with her finger, her faerie magic instantly solving it. "Zero point seven-seven seconds. A new record!" cried Pope.

Marvin angrily grabbed the Rubik's Cube out of Pixie's hand and tossed it aside. "That's not important. Confession time," he said, entering the confessional on Pixie's side and closing the door.

Pope got in the other side and spoke, "Say 'forgive me Father for I have sinned.'"

"Skip," came Marvin's reply.

"Skip?"

"Skip," repeated Marvin.

"When was your last confession?"

Marvin answered for Pixie, "She's never done it."

Pope sighed, and unenthusiastically said, "Confess your sins."

"Skip," said Marvin, again.

"Skip the sins?"

"Ask her if she's sorry."

Pope was demoralized. "Are you sorry?"

Marvin smiled at Pixie and asked her, "Do you want to see Cleopatra?"

"Yes!" exclaimed Pixie, suddenly excited.

Marvin got what he wanted. He spoke to Pope through the criss-cross wooden lattice, "OK, she said yes. Now penance."

"This seems like a forced confession," protested the robot Pope.

"Tell her to be good," said Marvin, passing on the proposed debate.

"Be good," said Pope, dejected.

Marvin congratulated Pixie, "Congratulations, Pixie. Now you get a present."

Pixie smiled.

Marvin asked, "How would you like to go see the Smithsonian? Huh?"

Pixie frowned.

Marvin tried again, "What about the Museum of Natural History? It's part of it now."

Pixie looked down, sad.

"No? British Museum? The Louvre?"

Pixie was still sad.

Marvin swung for the fences, "Do you like baseball?"

Nope, apparently.

Pope decided to help from the other side of the confessional, "Say the double W."

"Willie World?" guessed Marvin.

"Willie World?" said Pixie, excited.

"You want to go to Willie World?" asked

Marvin.

"Willie World!" cried Pixie.

It was settled. Marvin smiled and exclaimed, "We're goin' to Willie World!"

Chapter 4: Quiz Challenge

Cleopatra's stylish gold cross necklace caught the eye of Etty as they both sat in the unmoving Mercedes, waiting for Khorndahgh to return with the limousine. "You don't have to wear that anymore," said the gorilla, his brain crystals glowing red with annoyance.

Cleopatra looked over her torn and dirty Versace dress. "You want me to walk around naked everywhere like Pixie?"

"Not that, that," answered Etty, pointing to the gold cross necklace.

"My necklace?"

"You don't have to wear it. I'm not saved."

"It goes with all my outfits," said Cleopatra. This was no lie. Cleopatra also wore the necklace as a trophy of her confessional victory over Pope.

Etty conceded. "Oh, I see. Apropos I suppose,

in your case. Like a bible salesman. Don't worry, your secret's safe with me."

Cleopatra didn't see the point of a religious debate with a monkey, so she skipped it, "Speaking of secrets, what's this about a secret compartment?"

"You didn't know?" asked Etty, surprised, the red in his brain crystals fading out.

Cleopatra was disappointed in herself. Had she known that Etty was referring to the glove box, she would not have been. "No. What was in it?"

"A book." Etty pulled out the partly burned copy of Agatha Christie's *Murder on the Orient Express* from his satchel.

"My book!" exclaimed Cleopatra.

"I was reading it to Pixie."

Cleopatra tried to take the book from the gorilla, but was having trouble prying it from his paws.

"We haven't finished it," said the ape.

"That's okay, I can read the rest to Pixie."

Despite her declaration, Cleopatra was having no easier time prying the book from Etty's clutches.

"Well, I kind of want to know how it ends," said Etty, attached to the paws, attached to the book.

Cleopatra was a bit peeved, and not just because Etty would not unhand the book. "Why were you reading Pixie a book about how to get away with murder?" she asked.

"He gets away with it?" said Etty, shocked. His crystals glowed with multicolored lights.

"He?"

Etty's brain crystals lit up red. "Shut up! Don't say another word."

Cleopatra didn't say any words, but she did manage to extract the book from Etty's now-feeble clutches.

"You ruined it. I would have figured it out," said Etty, extremely disappointed.

"It's not like you think," assured Cleopatra.

Etty was not assured. "When I solve it, it will mean nothing. Now I know it was the girl and she got away with it."

"Which girl?" asked Cleopatra.

"You know which girl, and now I do too, thanks to you."

"All of your conclusions about whodunnit are—"

"Shut up!" shouted the gorilla, right in Cleopatra's face.

After an uncomfortable silence, Cleopatra realized she couldn't hold a book and drive at the same time. She looked for a safe place to put the book, but found none. Etty's satchel seemed like the best place. She turned to the ape. "Can you hang onto this for me?"

"You're not smart," said Etty, ignoring her question.

"What?"

"You're not smart."

"I never said I was," responded Cleopatra, fairly.

Etty's crystals glowed with blue light. "By the way Pixie talked about you, I thought you were going to be the female version of Einstein."

"I don't even like bagels."

"Don't play dumb."

"I thought I *was* dumb."

"I didn't say you were dumb, I said you weren't as smart as Einstein."

"What about you?" asked Cleopatra.

Etty's brain crystals glowed with blacklight. "Ha!" There was a time when Etty wasn't sure if he were smarter than Cleopatra, based on what Pixie told him.

"Okay, I challenge you," said Cleopatra.

"To what? A fashion contest?"

"Quiz Challenge."

Etty was surprised that Cleopatra was not even smart enough to know that she was not as smart as he. "Are you sincerely propounding that you have the perspicacity to vanquish *my* chordatan encephalon?"

"I think so," said Cleopatra, a bit confused by Etty's question. Cleopatra was not sure she could win this one, like she did the confession.

Overtaken by her ego, and hungry for a challenge, she ignored Sun Tzu's advice, "Yes?"

"Game on," said the ape, satisfied.

"Okay."

"What are we playing to?" asked Etty, rightfully concerned about the rules of this Quiz Challenge.

"One?"

Etty gave Cleopatra a look, his brain crystals glowing red.

Cleopatra relented, "Okay, two." She sat perfectly still, like a spider watching a fly buzzing nearby, confident that the game had already turned in her favor.

"Ten," said the ape.

"I don't have ten questions. Three."

"It has to be at least five," insisted Etty.

"Four."

"I said 'at least five.'"

"It's called a deal. You have to compromise," said Cleopatra.

"I thought it was a Quiz Challenge."

"Quiz Challenge to four."

Etty sighed.

Cleopatra took that as a 'yes.' "Deal!"

"Go ahead, ask your question," said the gorilla.

"Ladies first."

"Go ahead," said Etty, again.

"Ladies *answer* first." Cleopatra knew what she was doing.

Etty was already frustrated and not a single question had been asked. "Fine. What was the capital of Canada?"

"That's not fair."

"Why not?"

"There is no Canada."

"I said, 'was.'"

Cleopatra conceded to Etty's past-tense manifesto and thought really hard. She crescendoed her answer with a bad French accent, "It can only be beautiful Moo-Ree-All."

Cleopatra's answer and terrible French accent put Etty in a better mood. His brain crystals glowed with blacklight. He countered with a good Canadian accent, "Oh-duh-wuh."

"Never heard of it."

Like Cleopatra, Etty pronounced the Canadian Sin City's name with a French accent, but unlike Cleopatra, a near perfect one, "And Moo-ree-Ah-leh isn't beautiful anymore."

"Why would anyone nuke Canada?" wondered Cleopatra.

"Everyone nuked Canada."

"Half point," claimed Cleopatra.

"Why?"

"Montréal's in Canada. I was close."

"You don't get a half-point for a wrong answer."

Cleopatra relented, "Fine." This was going to be tougher on the answering end of it, she thought, but she also knew some things that the ape couldn't possibly know. She came out swinging, "Who painted the Sistine Chapel?"

"Michelangelo."

Cleopatra was disappointed. "How did you

know that?"

"I'm smart."

"Oh, right. One-one."

"Etty corrected her, "One-zero." Who was the first man on the moon?"

Cleopatra knew this one, as she had seen the movie. "Tom Hanks."

"Wrong. Neil Armstrong."

"Are you sure?"

"Yes. Tom Hanks was not an astronaut, and Apollo 13 never even made it to the moon. Still one-zero. Ask."

Cleopatra asked what she thought was a tough one, "What historical figure gave all her cakes to her adoring subjects so they wouldn't starve to death?"

Etty felt that he deserved a clue given the absurdity of the question. "Let them eat cake?"

"That's what *she* said," responded Cleopatra, laughing in her head.

"Marie Antoinette," answered Etty.

"How did you know?"

"She didn't give cake to people to stop them from starving." Etty was still unhappy about the premise of the question, even though he had won the vital clue.

Cleopatra protested, "She said, 'Let them eat cake!'"

"It would be like me calling you Aristotle."

Cleopatra understood. "She was trolling them."

"I suppose that's the correct parlance from the Age of Insanity," said the ape.

Cleopatra felt bad for Marie Antoinette. "Her majesty seemed like a pretty nice girl. I'm sure she didn't do it on purpose."

"That's what *she* said," replied Etty, laughing in his head.

"What happened to her?"

"Her 'adoring' subjects chopped off her head with a guillotine," revealed Etty.

"Oh. Two-one."

Etty corrected her again, "Two-zero. Who was the greatest conqueror in history?"

Cleopatra, being of Macedonian lineage, knew this one, "Alexander the Great."

Etty sounded the game show buzzer, "Ehnh, Napoleon."

"The short guy?"

Etty learned her, "He wasn't short for his time. And Napoleon won over fifty battles, far more than anyone else."

"What about Waterloo?" countered Cleopatra.

"That only counts as one loss."

"Alexander didn't lose any."

Etty could play the game within a game. "He didn't fight many."

Marvin's love of numbers was of some use to Cleopatra in this moment. "Alexander has the highest per-battle analytics rating."

Etty knew that analytics was like statistics, and he had read Mark Twain. "That would be like batting once in the majors, hitting a single, then retiring and being credited as the all-time batting champion."

"That's a good idea," said Cleopatra, thinking

that it was.

"It's not a good idea."

"Analytics. Half point."

Etty's sense of fairness was overtaken by impatience. "Fine."

"Yes! One to one-half."

"Two to one-half. Ask."

"How many Trojans did Brad Pitt kill?"

"Zero," answered Etty.

"Wrong. He killed lots. I saw it."

"That wasn't real."

"He beat up Bruce Lee."

"That was a movie." Etty hadn't seen the movie, but he did read about it. As it turns out, perhaps not surprisingly, much of the surviving literature from the Age of Insanity was movie-related.

"What about the Manson family?" said Cleopatra.

"Same movie."

"Those Nazis in the basement? Hitler!"

Etty brought the argument back to the

question. "There haven't been any Trojans around for millenia, and I'm pretty sure Brad Pitt never fought anyone."

"Oh, right. His face. Two to one-half."

"Three to one-half."

As Cleopatra waited for the next question, she questioned her own decision to play this game. Annoyed by the possibility that she made a mistake, and getting no question, she mocked the gorilla, "Aaaaaaask."

"I'm thinking," said the ape.

"I thought you were smart."

"I'm trying to think of an easy question."

"I'm sorry, take all the time you need." At this turn of events, Cleopatra regained hope, and her composure. As she waited for Etty's 'easy' question, she started calculating. "Ask me what the capital of America is."

Etty corrected her question, stating, "What *was* the capital of the *United States* of America."

"Washington!"

Etty conceded the ill-gotten point, "D.C.,

congratulations."

"Yes! One and a half. Now ask me where Seattle is."

"That's two questions."

"Lightning round."

Etty rolled his eyes, but decided to throw the dumb girl a life preserver, "Where is Seattle?"

"Washington! Two and a half. Now ask me who managed the Yankees."

"How many questions do you get?"

"Last one." Cleopatra was making some real headway, but she didn't want to push it.

Etty could see where this was going. "Who led the American revolutionary army?"

Cleopatra was already there. "Washington! Three and a half, I'm smarter than you."

Etty was still confident. "I haven't gotten my lightning round. Three questions. Ask."

"Let's make a deal."

Etty thought it had already been established that he wasn't dumb. "Why would I make a deal with *you*?"

"One question for one-hundred points."

"I don't need a hundred points, I only need one out of three."

"You'll have the Quiz Challenge record!" exclaimed Cleoptra, excited, like a game show contestant.

"There's no such thing as a Quiz Challenge record."

"There is now."

Etty was tired of all the rules lawyering and was still confident in the game they were supposed to be playing. He had, after all, answered every question correctly so far. He also wanted the Quiz Challenge record. "Fine. Ask."

Cleopatra had him. She knew Etty didn't know the answer to her next question and spared no discretion in flaunting her Nostradamian certainty of the fact. "How does z-point energy work?"

Etty didn't flinch but he did pause, then lazily circled his finger around in the air. He turned slowly to Cleopatra and answered the one-hundred point question, "Centrifuge spins around causing the mercury within to spin, creating a magnetic field that creates a warp bubble enclosing the craft. The space in front of the warp bubble is contracted, the space behind is expanded, propelling the craft through space-time like a flying saucer."

"Is that right?"

"You don't know the answer to your own question?"

"I didn't want it to be easy."

Etty claimed victory, "One-hundred three to three and a half. Game over. You lose."

"Did I?" said Cleopatra, as if she had meant to lose the Quiz Challenge as part of some grand scheme.

"Yes."

"By less than a hundred."

Etty gave Cleopatra a look, but secretly regretted the half point he gave her.

"Okay, so you're smarter than me. Who cares?" said Cleopatra, wanting to move on.

"Apparently *you* do. You're the one who challenged me to a battle of intellect."

"It doesn't matter."

"It does matter." It certainly did to Etty.

Cleopatra knew how to poke the gorilla. "Marvin's smarter than you, and I escaped his clutches."

"With our help."

"I could have escaped any time I wanted. I was just using Marvin for meals, entertainment, and indoor plumbing. But now that I know Pixie is alive..."

Etty looked into the future, "If we do rescue her, are you prepared to spend the rest of your life scavenging for food?"

Cleopatra was not. "No. We're gonna take down Marvin and get control of his robots. But first we need to rescue Pixie." Still holding the book in her hands, Cleopatra asked herself, "Where would Marvin take Pixie?"

Etty answered, "To his secret lair, obviously."

Cleopatra knew first hand that Marvin was

not stupid, but implied so of the ape, "Marvin isn't stupid. He doesn't have just *one* secret lair."

Etty unenthusiastically conceded the point, "Oh, yeah. I suppose that would be stupid."

Cleopatra flipped the pages of the Agatha Christie novel as she thought deeply. "She could be anywhere. What would Poirot say? Something about psychology…"

"I think he would state the obvious," suggested Etty. "Where was *your* prison cell, Mademoiselle?" he asked with his best French/Belgian accent.

"Prison cell?" said Cleopatra, puzzled.

"The room you were confined to."

"It was more of a complex."

"What? Riker's Island?"

"Versailles," admitted Cleopatra.

"The Palace of Versailles?"

"Well, it isn't *all* there."

"You lived in the Palace of Versailles?" said Etty, incredulous.

Cleopatra got defensive, as if she had been

accused of a crime. "Yeah, so? It wasn't all great. I mean, a lot of the rooms were being renovated."

Etty now understood, "Let them eat cake... Now I get it. You're not even as smart as I thought you were. I suppose you attended mass in the Sistine Chapel?"

"Yeah, so?"

"You're serious."

"I mean, not always. There are some really beautiful cathedrals that survived the apocalypse."

This decided it for Etty. "Too many churches. Versailles it is then."

Cleopatra dissented, "Marvin isn't stupid. He knows I know. He won't take her there."

Etty conceded, "Alright, a church then. So which one?"

"We're not attacking a church."

"Why not?"

"He'll take her to Versailles."

"You just said he wouldn't."

"It's a trap."

"Alright, so Versailles it is again," said Etty, wishing that she would just make up her mind.

"No. Too many robots. It's too dangerous. Pixie might get hurt."

"So where then?"

"He'll take her on a date."

Given past experience and Cleopatra's Quiz Challenge questions, Etty knew where Marvin took his dates. "The movies."

Cleopatra knew Pixie better than Etty knew Marvin. "No. Pixie's afraid of the dark. And you can't see her dress in the dark. And she can't sit through a movie."

"Where then?" asked Etty.

Cleopatra flipped the pages of the book again, trying to think like Poirot. "Psychology... He'll take her somewhere outside, during the day. Somewhere joyful, like the most joyful place in the world..."

Cleopatra and Etty turned to one another and both exclaimed, "Willie World!"

Chapter 5: Animatronics

Many years ago, in the pre-apocalyptic Age of Insanity, a nice family loaded with Willie World theme park gear sat in a small theme park boat made to look like a steamboat, slowly floating down a fabricated waterway.

As you know, Willie World was a world famous theme park located just outside of Tacoma, Washington. The park was dedicated to Steamboat Willie, a man-sized cartoon mouse who acted like a human. The boat floated into the Hall of Heroes, where the nice family floated past various animatronic heroes from history.

First up was an animatronic George Washington crossing the Delaware. The animatron emoted and eloquently spoke, "If freedom of speech is taken away, then dumb and silent we may be led like sheep to the slaughter.'"

After the Founding Father had his say, animatronic Abraham Lincoln, with a log cabin in the background, proclaimed with rugged eloquence, "America will never be destroyed from the outside. If we falter and lose our freedoms, it will be because we destroyed ourselves."

Next up was an animatronic Gandhi, a model of the Taj Mahal in the background. The animatron spoke with simple eloquence, "Be the change you wish to see in the world."

After Gandhi, there was a Reverend Martin Luther King Jr. animatron with a model of the Washington Monument and Lincoln Memorial Reflecting Pool in the background. The MLK animatron emoted and eloquently said, "I have a vision that my four small offspring will one day live in a country where they will not be subject to copyright laws that make it illegal to quote somebody's public speech."

Next up was an animatronic Neil Armstrong in a space suit with a model of the moon lander in the background. The animatron spoke with the voice of an everyman, tinged with the crackle of interplanetary communications, yet still with the eloquence of past eras as it emoted and misquoted, "That's one small step for man, one giant leap for mankind."

Next was a gaggle of animatronic women from history, behind them a model of the Statue of Liberty. The animatronic historical women all spoke in unison, so as to make their voices heard, "We did good stuff too!"

After the historical animatronic women made their voices heard, animatronic Tom Brady had his say. In the background was a display shelf made to look like a football goal post loaded with trophies. Gone was the eloquence of past figures as the animatronic Tom Brady spoke without sympathy, "If you don't play to win, don't play at all."

Finally, there was an animatron in the form of legendary daredevil Evel Knievel on a stunt bike, dressed in Evel's iconic red, white and blue star-spangled jump suit, against the backdrop of the Grand Canyon rocket launch stunt. The model rocket fired into the air, then fell straight down into the abyss. In a return to the eloquent speech of bygone eras, the Evel Knievel animatron spoke the eternal words, "Chicks dig scars."

The nice family's little steamboat floated out of the Hall of Heroes, along the artificial waterway, then into the Hall of Zeroes. First up in the ranks of infamy was an animatronic Emperor Nero, which fiddled while a model of Rome burned in the background. As the Nero animatron lovingly played its fiddle, it lamented, "Hidden talents count for nothing."

Next up was animatronic Osama bin Laden. In the background was a model of the World Trade Center buildings being hit by model airplanes, causing the twin towers to burst into flames and descend into the ground. The model reset and repeated the unspeakable crime again and again. Osama proclaimed, "I don't want to die humiliated or deceived."

After Osama, there was an animatronic Joseph Stalin. A model of the Kremlin stood behind the communist machine. Stalin spoke, "Death is the solution to all problems. I solved nine million problems."

Next up was a feisty Mao Tse-tung animatron, a model of the Great Wall of China in the background. The robotic Chairman Mao addressed the Stalin animatron with a terrible, thick, over-the-top asian accent, which had become popular after the song "I'm so Ronery" by Trey Parker won ten Grammys, printed here only for posterity's sake, "Onery nine mirrion? You carr that a genracide? I kirred hundred mirrion!"

Animatronic Stalin was stung by this remark, but animatronic Osama Bin Laden came to the rescue, "Oh, come on, it was eighty million at best."

Animatronic Mao was ready to tussle, "Oh, OK, mrister-died-in-his-knrickers after kirring mere trousands. You're not even in the mirrion crub. Why are you even hrere?"

Animatronic Nero sided with Osama, saying, "It's not just about how many were killed, it's about *how* they were killed. I burned an entire city of people. Style points. And what about hidden talents?" Animatronic Nero played its fiddle some more, exposing its hidden talent.

As the theme park steamboat stalled in the fake river, animatronic Pope Sixtus the Fourth put in its two bronze asses, or 'cents' in the modern parlance, "When do I get a turn?" Behind the Pope Sixtus animatron was a model of Joan of Arc being burned at the stake.

Animatronic Mao wasn't finished, "I hraven't sraid my qrote yet."

Animatronic Stalin, still stung by Chairman Mao's earlier criticisms, lamented to the little communist dictator, "I thought we were friends."

"Srerve the preprol!" cried animatronic Mao, finally getting its quote in.

"Can I go now?" asked animatronic Pope

Sixtus the Fourth.

"I got a rot mrore," answered animatronic Mao.

Animatronic Sixtus ignored Mao, and took its turn, "I am Pope Sixtus the Fourth, and I built the Sistine Chapel!"

Animatronic Mao called out Sixtus, "Oh, nrotice how he droesn't mrention the Spranish Inquisisron. Ret me gress, you kirred trousands! Oh, trousands! What a rot! I kirr mirrions."

Animatronic Stalin hated Pope Sixtus the Fourth, as you might have guessed, and offered, "I vote we kick the pope out. I mean, Sixtus the Fourth? Jesus Christ, make up your mind. Are you a six or a four?"

Chairman Mao answered, "He's a run wren it cromes to kirring preprol. I vrote hrim off!" The animatronic Mao put its vote hand up, followed by Stalin and Osama. They all looked at Nero, still playing the fiddle, whose hand was not yet raised.

Animatronic Nero explained its nay vote,

"Have you seen the Spanish Inquisition? Now that's a hidden talent!"

The Nero animatron played its fiddle again as animatronic Stalin gave Sixtus the bad news, "Three-one, you're gone."

Animatronic Pope Sixtus the Fourth objected, "You're a bunch of commies, it's not fair!"

Animatronic Stalin observed, "This is a democracy. Three-one, you lose."

"What about my vote?" asked Sixtus.

"It's the people who count the votes that matter," responded animatronic Stalin.

Pope Sixtus the Fourth appealed, "Well, what does Hitler have to say?"

The animatronic Adolf Hitler stood before the real Adolf Hitler's early artwork, which was propped up on easels. A sign next to the paintings read, 'Hitler's Hidden Talent'.

Sweat flew from animatronic Hitler's overly-animated head as it wagged its animatronic finger in the air and screamed, "Diese Lamm ist so unterkocht, dass es Mary zur Schule folgt!

Hier ist genug Knoblauch, um jeden Vampir in Europa zu töten! Hey, Panini-Kopf, hörst du mir überhaupt zu? Ich würde dir nicht einmal zutrauen, ein Bad einzulassen, geschweige denn ein Restaurant zu führen!"

Not knowing such hate was possible, Animatronic Stalin exclaimed, "Jesus Christ, he hates everyone!"

Animatronic Mao, a devout communist, was not a fan of religious terminology, even when used to curse. "Stop sraying 'Jesrus Christ!'"

Animatronic Pope Sixtus the Fourth, who was adverse to religious blasphemy, added, "I second that!"

Stalin dug at Sixtus the Fourth again, "Which is it? Second, sixth, or fourth? Make up your mind already!"

Mao claimed, "Hitrer onery kirr sixteen mirrion. I kirr hundred mirrion."

Animatronic Osama bin Laden disputed Chairman Mao's claims again, "Eighty, and those were mostly starvation deaths. That hardly even counts."

"A wrin is a wrin!" argued Mao.

Pope Sixtus got religious on them, "Me and Hitler killed God's chosen people. They count a lot more than chinamen. What are there, like a billion of 'em? You hardly made a dent. And according to Rasmussen, Hitler is the undisputed most evil person in history. He beat out the Devil, for Christ's sake!" Sixtus did not regret the blasphemy.

Animatronic Hitler had something important to scream about it, "Diese Pizza ist so ekelhaft, wenn du sie nach Italien nimmst, wirst du verhaftet! Das ist keine Pizza, das ist ein Fehler!" Animatronic Hitler continued its rant, but you get the point.

Back in the present, which is to say the future, meaning the post-apocalypse, the Hitler animatron stood motionless, dusty and cobwebbed. The Hall of Zeroes was in ruins, the artificial waterway dried up.

Rising up the wall was a large, hunched over

shadow of a man wearing a wide-brimmed hat, the same as in Umbatu's death dream. His evil eyes glowing red, the Hat Man moved his shadowy claw-fingers towards the animatronic Hitler and laughed demonically. As the Hat Man clawed at the fascist machine, there was a spark, and the animatron stood up straight. The demonic laughter of the Hat Man faded away as his shadowy form descended from this world.

Hitlerbot immediately began screaming nonsense, its overly-animated head sending sweat flying as it waved its finger in the air demonstrably, "Dieser Fisch ist so roh, dass er immer noch Nemo sucht! Du hast so viel Öl verwendet, die USA wollen den verdammten Teller überfallen!"

A nearby battalion of Nazibots were inspired into a frenzy of hate by Hitlerbot's speech. The fascist footsoldiers were originally animatronic automatons from the Alabama Smith Tomb Robber Adventure Ride at Willie World. They were built in the form of steampunk Nazis, complete with gas masks and steampunk weapons, and now given robot life by the Hat Man. The Nazibot mockeries of human life gave Hitler the Nazi salute and shouted in unison, "Heil Hitlerbot!"

Chapter 6: The Present

Etty was trying to remove the ignition switch casing on the Mercedes-Benz 300 SL Roadster supercar, but the tools from the limousine that Khorndahgh had wheeled over were not working. His brain crystals glowed with blacklight as he continued trying with determined enthusiasm.

Cleopatra sat with Khorndahgh in the back of the white 1959 Cadillac Fleetwood 75 converted stretch limousine, dining on leftover caviar and champagne. Khorndahgh refused the champagne but gulped down the fish eggs. "It's good,' he said.

"It's raw eggs," said Cleopatra.

"Protein," said Khorndahgh, before washing down the caviar with the melted ice from the fancy champagne bucket.

"Wanna play checkers?" asked Cleopatra.

"I'm the Checker King!" said Khorndahgh, excited.

"Let's play!"

Khorndahgh frowned. "Forgot the checkers at Fishy's house."

"Have you ever lost?" asked Cleopatra, curious about his match with Etty.

"I'm the Checker King!" said Khorndahgh, again.

"So you beat Etty?"

Khorndahgh couldn't talk about it. "First rule of checkers is don't talk about it."

"What's the second rule?" asked Cleopatra, amused.

"Second rule of checkers is don't talk about it."

"Sounds a lot like the first rule."

"First rule of checkers is don't talk about it," repeated Khorndahgh.

"Maybe we can play something else."

"Boulder throw?"

"Truth or dare."

Khorndahgh didn't tell Cleopatra, but he was also the truth or dare champion, which you know unless you're reading these books out of order. "Dare!" he said.

Cleopatra dared, "I dare you to tell me about Etty v Khorndahgh checkers."

"Khorndahgh v Gorilla."

"Yeah, that."

Khorndahgh conceded the match, "You win."

Cleopatra was not trying to win. "I withdraw the question."

"You can't do that."

"Have you read the rules of truth or dare?" asked Cleopatra.

The barbarian admitted, "Khorndahgh don't read."

Cleopatra was good at making up rules. "Truth or dare rule eight, section two-B, 'The questioner may withdraw the question if it's unfair.'"

"Question fair. You win," said Khorndahgh, accepting the ruling.

Cleopatra gave up on truth or dare, seeing it as an unfortunate loss. She changed gears, "Let's arm wrestle."

"OK," said Khorndahgh. The barbarian easily won the contest of strength, though taking great care not to break her arm.

"You win," said Cleopatra, glad that he didn't break her arm.

"That was too easy," said Khorndahgh, disappointed.

Cleopatra thought of something more fun, "Do you have Twister?"

"Can't carry a tornado in your pants."

"Are you sure?"

"No. Never tried."

Cleopatra looked at the gigantic fiery sun, now high in the sky. It was getting warm in the limousine. "Mud wrestling?"

"Might hurt you."

"John Cougar said it feels good."

"It won't."

Cleopatra turned up the heat, "They wrestled

naked in the Olympics."

"Khorndahgh don't need clothes."

"Who does? Is Pixie your girlfriend?"

"Czary."

Cleopatra didn't know exactly what to make of that remark, but took it as a 'no.' "Do you have a girlfriend?" she asked.

"Lots."

"Haven't found the right one?"

"Khorndahgh mate must bear children stronger than Khorndahgh," said the barbarian.

"What about smarter?"

"Khorndahgh smart enough."

"Cheers to that, kemosabe."

Khorndahgh was a barbarian, and he said so, "Khorndahgh barbarian."

"German?"

"Khorndahgh Polish."

"Like the sausage?"

"The big one."

Cleopatra put her hand on Khorndahgh's abdominal wound dressing made from the ripped-off portion of her Versace dress. "Let me take a look." She began to undo the wrapping. When she got to the skin layer the dressing stuck to the wound, glued with dried blood. "Count to ten."

"One..."

Cleopatra ripped off the Versace wound dressing like it was a bandaid.

"Two..." said Khorndahgh without flinching. "What's next?"

"Ten," answered the Macedonian siren.

"Ten."

Cleopatra felt the Scorpionbot stinger wound, now almost entirely healed. "It's almost entirely healed."

"I heal fast."

Cleopatra moved her hand up Khorndahgh's muscled chest, impressed by the specimen. She looked right into Khorndahgh's eyes, her own aflutter. "You're so strong."

Khorndahgh kissed her and they started making out. As it began to get hot and heavy, the estrous young woman initiated a leg straddle.

"What are you doing?" said Etty, now by the open window, his crystals aglow with green light.

Cleopatra paused the make-out session only long enough to answer, "Makin' out."

"Well stop it!"

Cleopatra and Khorndahgh continued making out.

Etty knew what to say, "C'mon, break it up. We have to save Pixie."

Cleopatra slowly disengaged from Khorndahgh and wiped her mouth. "Don't be jealous," she said to the ape.

"I'm not jealous."

"That's not what your headlight says."

"My what?"

Cleopatra explained, "The light in your crystals. Red is pouting, blue is humiliated, purple is emotionally distant...I'm pretty sure green is envy. Marvin made it easy."

Etty was stunned. His brain crystals glowed with a multitude of colors. "There's a light in my crystals?"

"You didn't know?"

"No, I—"

"I shouldn't have said anything," said Cleopatra, disappointed in herself for losing the advantage.

Etty's crystals glowed with blue light. "You're not a good person."

"Maybe. How did you not know? You can't see the light?"

Etty had multiple theories, but chose the easiest one to explain, "I thought it was the Multapocalyptic Atmospheric Lensing Effect. You don't see colored lights in your periphery sometimes?"

"Just yours. I wonder why they didn't tell you."

"You know why."

"They're nice?"

Etty's crystals turned red. "They're stupid!"

Khorndahgh sat unmoving in the limousine, unoffended and disinterested. The barbarian didn't care about words. Arguments were best settled by combat.

Cleopatra liked words, and arguing with fools. She also loved her sister. "Pixie's not stupid. She saved us all with her faerie magic."

Etty credited himself, "I told her to make those things."

"What about Khorndahgh? He orders you all over the battlefield."

"You weren't there."

Cleopatra remembered being there. "I was in a balloon, above, with a bird's-eye view."

"You couldn't hear us talking."

"Being smart isn't just about saying big words."

The gorilla's brain crystals glowed with blacklight, which, of course, is the color purple. "I'm cognizant of that actuality."

"See, that's what I'm talking about."

Etty's crystals turned red again. "What about you?"

"I never said I was smart. You did."

Etty became angrier. "Not that. You knew about my headlight this whole time and didn't tell me. You were using it against me." Etty's crystals dimmed to blue. "You're an even worse person than I thought," he said, regretfully.

"Would an even worse person get you a present?" asked Cleopatra.

"You got me a present?"

"Yeah."

Etty looked around the desert wasteland, his brain crystals turning red again. "Where? The invisible present store?"

"Yeah."

The gorilla's crystals glowed with blacklight. "Alright, well where is it?"

"In the limo," revealed Cleopatra.

"Where in the limo?"

"In the glove box."

"You got me gloves?"

"No, that's just what they call it."

Etty's crystals turned red. "There's not a glove box in the limousine."

By now Cleopatra had surmised that the 'secret compartment' was, in fact, the glove box. "You call it a secret compartment."

"Why would people keep gloves in the secret compartment?" asked the gorilla.

"You don't know how valuable gloves are. You don't need 'em."

Etty's crystals glowed with blacklight as he stared at his paws. He got into the passenger seat of the limousine with no door to stop him, and almost pushed the button on the secret compartment. His crystals turned yellow. "Is something going to pop out at me?"

Cleopatra didn't think so. "I don't think so."

Etty pushed the button and the glove box popped open. Stuffed inside was the white cowboy hat that Khorndahgh wore at the Battle of the Pyramid Mound. The gorilla's crystals glowed red. "Oh, very funny. Now Khorndahgh's going to wear it everywhere, and I'm going to have to endure it." His brain crystals glowed blue again. "You're an even worse person than the worse person I thought you were."

"It's not for him, it's for you."

"Why?"

Cleopatra was surprised that Etty didn't get it. "Every man's deepest fear is having his emotions broadcast to the world."

"I'm not a man."

Cleopatra disagreed. "That's debatable."

"No, it's not."

Cleopatra was disappointed that her gift went unappreciated. "Well anyway, I got you the hat if you want to hide your headlight.

"Khorndahgh isn't going to let me have it." Etty was sure of it.

"He said he would," said Cleopatra.

Etty glanced at Khorndahgh again, who was smiling.

Cleopatra continued, "On one condition."

"What? I have to follow his orders?"

"No, you just have to wear it."

Etty glanced at Khorndahgh again, who was still smiling. The ape's crystals glowed with pink light as he turned back to Cleopatra. "Well that's the point of it, isn't it?" Etty looked down at the hat, unsure if he wanted to be Khorndahgh's clown.

"Be a man. Put on the hat," said Cleopatra.

Etty's brain crystals glowed with blacklight as he held the hat in his left paw and looked at his empty right paw, thinking deeply.

Cleopatra spoke dramatically, "In one hand, his emotions exposed to the world. In the other, a cowboy hat."

Etty put on the hat.

Khorndahgh's smile widened. "Looks good," he said.

Cleopatra claimed victory, "I told you you were a man."

Appreciating the gift and its intent, Etty felt bad about what he said before. "You're not a bad person."

The cowboy hat was a JW Brooks, of such quality that Corruptsheriffbot's Chinese bullet could not penetrate it. It had taken Cleopatra a lot of effort to make the 'bullet hole', due to the quality of the brand. Cleopatra glanced at the blue light visible through the 'bullet hole' in the cowboy hat. "How's that humble pie taste?" she said.

"What about you?" asked the gorilla, referring to Cleopatra's Quiz Challenge defeat.

"No time. Gotta save Pixie."

Chapter 7: Willie World

As you know, Willie World was not Marvin's first attempt at a theme park. Before the robot cowboys at Marvin's Wild West World theme park went haywire and started attacking the guests, Marvin had built Cretaceous Park, which, unlike some other dinosaur parks, was chronologically accurate, though the dinosaurs were robots instead of computer-generated images. Of course, just like the other dino parks, the dinosaurs broke loose from their enclosures and began eating the guests.

Instead of building a completely new park, Marvin had decided to refurbish Willie World, which had been in existence since the mid-twentieth century. Willie World was Marvin's attempt to build a theme park that didn't try to murder its guests. The attempt would ultimately fail, as you will soon see.

Marvin and Pixie had, by now, arrived at Willie World. Marvin was having the park renovated with the intent of bringing Cleopatra there again once it was fully restored, as their previous visit was plagued by ride closures and no toilet paper in the restrooms. At this time, the theme park was still partly ruined, but adequate enough for Marvin's current purposes.

Marvin and Pixie were having a ride in Caroline Cow's Coffee Cups, which spun around each other in circles. Marvin was dressed as Prince Charming, with a regal outfit of white brocade, complete with a white baby seal fur mantle and white cape. A golden utility belt encircled his sizable waist, ringed with golden orbs holding various gadgets miniaturized by nano-shrink technology. Pixie was dressed as Tinker Bell, except that her faerie outfit was pink, and included magic faerie wings with the substance of projected images.

As the giant coffee cups spun around each

other, Pixie smiled and giggled. Marvin, on the other hand, was feeling sick. "I should decommission this ride," he said, holding his stomach and wishing he hadn't refurbished the Coffee Cups.

Exiting Caroline Cow's Coffee Cups, Marvin and Pixie walked over to Fairy Tale Castle. Pixie giggled and waved at the Willie World characters walking over to them. The characters were much like those played by actors when Willie World was originally in use, except they were now played by Actorbots. Not unlike their human predecessors, the Actorbots were prone to repetition.

Pixie was delighted. Marvin pulled an orb-shaped golden capsule from his utility belt and crushed it. An old Polaroid instant film camera de-miniaturized in his hand, which he used to snap a picture of Pixie standing with the Willie World characters in front of Fairy Tale Castle.

As Marvin stood there waving the picture in development to dry it out, he thought he spied something moving over by the Savage Mountain, which was a roller coaster built into a huge model of Mount Everest. He scanned the fake mountain for a bit, but saw nothing else. Probably an animal, he thought, but he put himself on yellow alert.

Moving on, Marvin and Pixie boarded King Baldwin's Crusader Carousel and rode upon some wooden crusader horses. Pixie giggled with joy, riding a white Templar horse. Marvin hung on tightly to a black French crusader horse, clenching his teeth as the wooden equine underneath him bobbed up and down as it went 'round and 'round. That's when the steampunk Nazibots attacked.

Marvin was expecting barbarians, not Nazibots. In any event, he was ready for the attack. He hopped off the crusader horse and activated a transparent aluminum shield from his utility belt just in time to block a steampunk flamethrower fire stream shot by a steampunk Nazibot. The shield deflected the fire into the carousel, setting some of the wooden horses aflame.

The flamethrower fire began melting Marvin's aluminum shield, and to make matters worse, Nazibots wielding chainsaw-axes were charging his flank. Marvin tossed a tactical EMP grenade from his utility belt to disable the flamethrowing Nazibot, then threw an acid grenade at the chainsaw-axe-wielding Nazibots. The acid began disintegrating the fascist robots as they closed in, and the machines fell to pieces before they could attack.

Marvin dropped the aluminum shield, which burst into flames from the heat. As the wooden horses on the carousel burned in a fiery equine cataclysm, he wondered aloud, "I didn't build any Nazibots. Where did they come from?"

After finishing his vocalized thought, Marvin saw another group of steampunk Nazibots charging from the other side of the carousel, wielding chainsaw-swords. He began to reach for his utility belt again, but before he could grab an orb, Pixie extended her arm towards the blazing stallions, using her faerie magic to make them spin sideways on their poles to block the Nazibot advance. The Nazibots had to cut through the burning wooden carousel horses with their chainsaw-swords, delaying them.

Taking advantage of the delay, Marvin pulled Pixie off her horse and they raced to the Imbecile Elephant ride. Being that Marvin and Pixie were the park's only guests, the Actorbots followed them in a jolly procession. Marvin wasn't going to let a few Nazis ruin the date, so he and Pixie boarded a fiberglass Imbecile Elephant named Stupido and proceeded down the dusty, hay-strewn track.

From a golden orb on his utility belt, Marvin extracted a control box labeled 'ACTORS', and pushed the big red button. The Actorbots, costumed as various Willie World characters, sprang into action, blocking the Steampunk Nazibots that were converging upon the Imbecile Elephant ride. The Actorbots' hands mechanically transformed into the shapes of hammers and sickles.

An Actorbot in a Steamboat Willie outfit took the lead. Willie laughed a high-pitched, squeaky laugh and slashed a steampunk Nazibot's gas mask tube with a sickle attack, causing the Nazibot to fall to the ground and convulse like it was suffocating. Green gas shot wildly from the severed tube as the fascist robot writhed on the ground. After the sickle slash, Willie used its hammer-hand to fell a flanking Nazibot, smashing its gasmasked robot head in.

Another Nazibot with a chainsaw-axe came at Steamboat Willie. Willie laughed again and agilely tumbled backwards as an Actorbot playing Doofus Dog charged headlong into the Nazibot's chainsaw-axe, splitting the weird man-dog in half. Bisected by the chainsaw-axe, Doofus Dog fell to the ground in two halves.

The chainsaw-axe-wielding Nazibot was quickly run through by the antlers of Baby Deer's Mother, played by another Actorbot, after which

Baby Deer's Mother was shot dead by a blunderbuss-wielding steampunk Nazibot, which was then disintegrated by a bullet from an antimatter plasma .44 Magnum revolver that Marvin had extracted from an orb on his utility belt.

Baby Deer cried over its dead mother, the Actorbot inside the costume calling up all the emotional sadness of its robot life in order to give an Oscar-worthy performance, after which Baby Deer was accidentally disintegrated by the antimatter plasma .44 Magnum as Marvin blasted two more advancing Nazibots. "Sorry," said Marvin to Baby Deer's insoluble residue.

An Actorbot playing Flakey the Snowman spun around, the hammer and sickle on its wooden stick-arms bashing and slicing down nearby Nazibots. Before the Actorbot could do any more damage, Flakey's head was blown off by a steampunk cowboy Nazibot with a steampunk six-shooter.

The cowboy Nazibot holstered its six-shooter

and turned to an Actorbot playing the famous gunfighter Annie Oakley, waiting in a gunfight stance. The Nazibot drew first, but Annie was quicker on the draw! Unfortunately the Annie Oakley Actorbot did not have a gun in its holster due to the fact that Willie World was a theme park for children, and the character actors were not allowed to carry guns. Annie was repeatedly blasted by the cowboy Nazibot's steampunk six-shooter. The Nazibot, full of hatred, continued pulling the trigger after the bullets were spent, click click click.

The cowboy Nazibot was taken down by the hammers and sickles of Actorbots playing Duck and Goat from the *Steamboat Willie* cartoon, which were then trampled to death by a Zug of steampunk Nazibots charging from Fairy Tale Castle.

The Actorbot playing Steamboat Willie stood alone, but held its ground. Surrounded by the fascist mob, Willie ferociously slew Nazibot after Nazibot before going down, laughing a squeaky laugh as the Nazibots cut the robot mouse to pieces.

Still on the Imbecile Elephant ride with Pixie, Marvin disintegrated two more pursuing Nazibots with his revolver. Another Nazibot caught up to the fiberglass elephant and climbed up, raising its chainsaw-sword to attack.

Marvin's .44 Magnum revolver carried six antimatter plasma bullets when fully loaded, but in all the excitement Marvin wasn't sure if he had fired six shots or only five, so he threw the heavy gun at the Nazibot, hitting it squarely in its gasmasked face and knocking its head clean off. The headless robot fell to the track, terminated.

With more Nazibots in pursuit, Pixie waved her hands in the air, her faerie magic animating Stupido, which broke away from the ride and stampeded through the streets of Willie World. Stupido ran to the Savage Mountain roller coaster, carrying Pixie and Marvin. Once inside the coaster station, the elephant exploded into glitter, depositing the pair into a coaster cart made to look like a Himalayan goral, which is a goat-like deer that can easily traverse the difficult terrain of Mount Everest.

Marvin and Pixie screamed in terror as the roller coaster cart climbed upward, then screamed even louder as they dropped down the first hill. They weren't just screaming because of the drop, but also because of the steampunk Nazibot waiting for them at the bottom of the hill. Marvin and Pixie ducked the Nazibot's chainsaw-sword blade as they whooshed by, the goral cart zooming upward and around the mountain after the drop, where more Nazibots were waiting for them.

Marvin pulled a golden orb from his utility belt and crushed it. A pump action double barreled pop-shotgun de-miniaturized in his hand. The shotgun fired electroballs, generated by the pump action, which Marvin used to blast a few Nazibots off the mountain. The robots' screams echoed through the mountain tunnels as they fell to their deaths.

Pixie conjured up a huddle of faerie penguins in the coaster cart's empty seat behind them. The penguins flew into the air to block the Nazibots' steampunk ranged attacks, exploding into icy glitter when hit by the crossbow bolts and blunderbuss slugs. Some of the faerie penguins flew right into the fascist robots and exploded into icy glitter bombs, freezing the Nazibots in casings of ice.

A steampunk Nazibot hiding in a mountain tunnel unleashed its flamethrower at the coaster cart. The remaining faerie penguins took flight, countering the firestream with icy breaths. But the fire was too strong. Engulfed by the flames, the penguins exploded into icy glitter. The icy glitter froze the fire, which fell onto an outcropping below and shattered.

Marvin produced a magnetron laser pointer from a utility belt orb and used it to slice off a few fake ice stalactites above the flamethrowing Nazibot, which was impaled and terminated by the falling ice-spikes.

Racing down, around, and through the mountain in their goral coaster cart, Marvin continued to blast steampunk Nazibots with his electroball pump action shotgun. Seeing the usefulness of faerie magic, he turned to Pixie and asked, "What else can you do?"

Pixie responded with a flash of her hands, magically changing from her Tinkerbell outfit into a Swiss Appenzeller dress. A flowery headband crowned her noggin.

Marvin was disappointed, and said as much, "Wrong mountain. And that doesn't help us."

To Marvin's surprise, the flowers in Pixie's headband began yodeling, creating a sonic resonance that deflected the crossbow bolts and blunderbuss slugs from the remaining Nazibots.

When they finally splashed down at the end of the ride, Pixie's dress exploded into musical glitter, and was replaced by a pink ballerina tutu.

After pocketing the laser pointer and holstering the shotgun in his belt, Marvin grabbed Pixie's hand and they exited the ride, dashing away from the pursuing Nazibots. Waiting for them at the ride's exit were more Actorbots, costumed as charming princes. The prince Actorbots covered Marvin and Pixie's escape, laying down their robot lives to protect the park's guests, unlike real theme park workers would.

Marvin and Pixie ran to the Storyland Steamboats, and hopped aboard. Not satisfied with the speed of the boats on the children's ride, Marvin extracted a battery-powered propeller from a utility belt orb. He dunked the propeller into the water, propelling the boat forward at a faster speed.

There was no tour guide to tell the stories of the little model houses and idyllic castles they passed, but Pixie used her faerie magic to fill it in with tiny dancing faerie animals dressed in pink tutus, just like her own.

Seeing no Nazinbots on this ride, Marvin was hopeful that the Actorbots had finished them off so that he could enjoy the rest of the date without interference. Unfortunately for Marvin, the steampunk Nazibots were merely regrouping for a final assault to be devised by their Führer.

As the theme park boat continued along the waterway, animatronic storybook characters began singing "Hey Jude" by The Beatles. When they got to the na-na-na-na part, Marvin became annoyed by the repetitiveness of it. "Does this song ever end?" he said, blasting the little animatronic characters with his shotgun to shut them up. This made Pixie cry.

Marvin apologized, "Sorry, I can't stand this song anymore," before blasting another one.

Pixie spoke through her tears, "I like this song."

Marvin kept blasting the singing puppets anyway, apologizing again and again until the chorus of voices became a single animatronic duck, quacking the refrain. Not wanting to upset Pixie further, Marvin spared the duck.

Chapter 8: Taking Flight

Etty was in the 300 SL, trying to remove the ignition switch casing. Still sitting in the limousine, Cleopatra asked the gorilla, "Did you get it?"

Etty stumbled, "Well, no. I mean, I can't..." then came up with an excuse, "I don't have the right tools."

"Let me try," said Cleopatra.

The pink light in Etty's hat-hole dimmed to red. "You'll fare no better."

Cleopatra wiped her brow with the back of her hand. "Khorndahgh, I'm feeling a bit faint from all your kisses. Can you carry me to the Mercedes?"

Etty spoke from the Mercedes, which was sitting next to the limousine. "It's right here!"

Khorndahgh carried Cleopatra to the 300 SL and gently placed her in the driver's seat. Cleopatra asked, "Khorndahgh, can you break open this keyhole without breaking the car?"

Khorndahgh leaned over Cleopatra and punched the ignition switch just right, causing the casing to break open, but doing no other damage to the car or its mechanisms.

"I did it!" exclaimed Cleopatra.

"We should have done that in the first place," said Etty, frustrated.

"I didn't think of it," admitted Cleopatra.

Neither did Etty, so he dropped the complaint.

Cleopatra reached into the broken keyhole and turned a switch, but nothing happened. "It's not working. What does the manual say about it?"

Etty glanced at the limousine. "I only read part of a Gremlin manual, and I only drove the limousine, which is an automatic."

"What's this other pedal for?" Cleopatra

stepped on the extra pedal a few times. "It doesn't do anything."

"Let me see." Etty adjusted his cowboy hat before speaking to Khorndahgh, who was still standing by the driver's side door next to Cleopatra, "Khorndahgh, in the caboose."

Khorndahgh looked around, confused.

Etty clarified, "Get in back."

After Khorndahgh got in the trunk, Etty snatched the Agatha Christie novel from Cleopatra's unsuspecting hands and put it into his satchel. "Press the third pedal and turn the ignition switch."

With the car in neutral, Cleopatra engaged the third pedal and turned the ignition switch. The supercar's gas engine rumbled to life, but only because Marvin had modified the 300 SL's ignition system so that it operated more like a modern automobile, without the need for a fuel pump switch or choke lever. "It worked!" said Cleopatra. "We make a good team."

Etty spoiled the camaraderie, "I could have

done it myself."

Cleopatra revved the engine, smiling like a sun devil. "Ready?"

"No," answered Etty.

Cleopatra put the pedal to the metal. The 300 SL's gas engine revved but the supercar went nowhere. She let off the gas.

"Release the third pedal," suggested Etty.

Cleopatra let off the third pedal and the car died. "You killed it."

"Why would it... It's a clutch. Why would they put it there?"

"What does the manual say?" asked Cleopatra.

Etty answered, "It was an automatic manual... Manual! The clutch is there to shift the gears manually."

"It doesn't work."

Etty pawed at the gear shifter. "That's what this stick is for. Start the car again." After Cleopatra started up the Roadster again, Etty continued, "Now keep your foot on the clutch and shift gears with this stick. Try 1st gear."

"Marvin used 8th gear," said Cleopatra.

"That's an infinity symbol," explained Etty.

"This is a Mercedes, not an Infinity. And this number is clearly an eight." Cleopatra switched to '8th gear' and hit the gas. The engine revved again but the car still went nowhere.

Etty instructed, "Slowly let off the clutch and press the gas very lightly."

Cleopatra did as instructed, but awkwardly, causing the supercar to lurch forward and die again.

"Maybe we need to be in the air," suggested Etty.

"This knob." Cleopatra pointed to the red 'CVLS' flat knob.

"What is 'CVLS'?" asked Etty.

Cleopatra tried to pronounce the strange word, "CaVLeS? CiVoLuS? CoVeLiS? I'm gonna need to buy a vowel."

Etty thought and said, "It's an acronym. L is for levitate."

"Or lift," suggested Cleopatra.

Etty was sure, "It's levitate. Levitation System. CV... It should be AG. Anti-Gravity Levitation System. Why is it CV? Maybe it's not antigravity. Maybe it uses thrusters. What kind of thrusters would be called CV?"

Cleopatra remembered, "It wasn't thrusters, it was like a balloon."

Etty didn't see it that way, "A balloon? To lift this vehicle with passengers would require a balloon the size of the Hindenburg."

Cleopatra was becoming impatient. "There's no balloon, it just floats like one. Anyway, who cares how it works as long as it works."

"I do."

"We're short on time."

Etty was persuaded. "Start the car."

Cleopatra started the engine and pulled the red CVLS flat knob, which engaged the Condensed Vacuum Lift System. The supercar floated up into the air like a balloon, but was unstable. The car tilted upward and air blasts shot out from below, pushing the vehicle backwards. Etty and Khorndahgh were thrown out, but caught themselves and hung from the tilted car. Etty's cowboy hat fell off revealing his brain crystals, which glowed yellow with terror.

Cleopatra found the ball knob joystick near the shifter and leveled the supercar as Etty and Khorndahgh climbed back in. The gorilla tried to look up at his crystals, but could guess their color. "I fear what's next," he said.

Cleopatra used the control knob to descend to the cowboy hat. Like a center fielder running to a fly ball, she yelled, "I got it!" then opened the door and grabbed the cowboy hat. After closing the door again she placed the hat back on Etty's head and said, "Your fear is gone."

Seeing the fear in the ape's eyes, as well as his hat-hole, Cleopatra took a little time to practice. She used the ball knob joystick to ascend and tilt the car in various ways so as to make it fly, after which she leveled the floating supercar, which gently swayed like a boat on a lake.

Etty was pleased, his hat-hole light extinguished. "We can fly."

"Not fast enough," worried Cleopatra.

Etty had hope. "Alright, what did Marvin do next?"

"Centrifuge," answered Cleopatra.

"Probably the red rocker switches," posited Etty.

"Sammy Hagar?"

Etty pointed to the red rocker switches. "Those three."

Cleopatra looked at the three switches. "Which one?"

"All of them, I assume."

"Why are there three? Shouldn't there just be one?"

Etty postulated, "They're probably for different systems within the system. Push them one at a time. I thought you saw Tom Hanks do this."

"I wasn't watching his hands." Cleopatra pushed down the red rocker switches one at a time, and they lit up orange. The sound of a bubble gum bubble being blown was heard as the warp bubble materialized around the car. She looked at the silver disk-shaped centrifuge on the hood of the car, which did not appear to be spinning. "The centrifuge isn't spinning."

"It *is* spinning. It's just hard to see. What next?"

Cleopatra pointed at the z-point accelerator lever. "This thing." She pulled the lever and the navigation screen lit up. The supercar's engine rumbled with the whirring, pulsating sound of a flying saucer.

Etty pointed at the navigation screen. "Navigation..."

Cleopatra pounced, "I'll do it."

"Are you sure?"

"Yeah, I know this part." Cleopatra turned the dials to set the navigation. "Now the top speed, mach one-hundred." Cleopatra punched in mach one-hundred on the keypad.

Etty protested, "We're not starting at mach

one-hundred." Etty pointed to a button on the keypad. "See here, kilometers per hour. Let's go with ten kilometers per hour." Punching numbers on the keypad, he changed the top speed to ten kilometers per hour.

"I'm not a granny. One-hundred." Cleopatra changed the top speed to one-hundred kilometers per hour.

Etty compromised, "Fifty-five." Etty changed the top speed to fifty-five kilometers per hour.

"I can't drive fifty-five."

"Fifty-six, then."

"Mach fifty-six." Cleopatra changed the top speed to Mach 56.

"We're not starting at mach speed."

"Sammy Hagar would," argued Cleopatra.

"No, he wouldn't. He drank and drove responsibly."

"He drank tequila."

Cleopatra and Etty argued for a while as Khorndahgh sat in the trunk, bored. A lone bird cried out, and still they argued. A coyote howled, and the argument continued. When the argument finally ended, they sat in silence as the floating supercar swayed in the air. Etty adjusted his white cowboy hat.

Breaking the awkward silence, Cleopatra went down the checklist, "Okay, balloon blown. Centrifuge fuging. This thing is up. Map set. Mach fifty-six after that unnecessary Sammy Hagar discussion. Stick in eighth gear. Warp bubble bubbling..." Cleopatra flipped up the four toggle switches. "All systems go. Ready?"

"Punch it lightly," said the ape.

Cleopatra let off the clutch and put the pedal to the metal. The floating supercar skidded, then zoomed away like a flying saucer. The view from the supercar moving at mach fifty-six was like the view from a supersonic jet flying at low altitude, but much faster.

"Why is there a breeze?" asked Etty, annoyed by it.

"We're flying," Cleopatra told the stupid monkey.

"We're in a warp bubble. There shouldn't be anything at all."

"Oh. Marvin must've added it."

"Why?" asked Etty, not seeing the logic in it.

"It's more fun this way."

Etty saw ruins ahead. "Slow down."

"How?"

"Let off the gas pedal." Etty punched in some numbers on the keypad. "Reducing top speed. Sorry, Sammy."

Cleopatra spied the bent Space Needle ahead in the ruins of Seattle. "Willie World!"

"That's not Willie World. That's the Space Needle," said Etty.

"Willie World Space Needle."

A red light appeared in Etty's hat-hole. He pointed off to the south. "Willie World is over there, by Tacoma. Your navigation is wrong. You should have let me do it."

"Yeah," said Cleopatra, pretending to be dumb.

Etty was happy to take over. "Not a problem.

I'll just fix it."

"Wait."

"Why?"

"I have to use the ladies' room."

Etty pointed in the direction of Willie World. "There are restrooms at Willie World. It's right over there."

"You haven't used the restrooms at the Museum of Pop Culture. They're spectacular. Willie World is always out of toilet paper." Avoiding a protracted argument, Cleopatra flew the supercar down to the ruins of the Museum of Pop Culture, which sat next to the bent Space Needle. The Pop Museum had been partly renovated by Marvin, who had re-digitized the featured music from analog sources, mainly old vinyl records.

As Etty was waiting for Cleopatra to use the ladies' room, he was sampling some rock n' roll music in the ruined museum. The gorilla was wearing headphones, upside down under his chin so as not to interfere with his cowboy hat, and listening to Led Zeppelin.

Cleopatra walked up with a book in hand. She was now clean and with a fresh coat of makeup, dressed in Gerri Halliwell's Union Jack dress, having just pilfered it from the museum. She spoke to Etty, but he couldn't hear her with the headphones on.

Seeing Cleopatra speaking, the gorilla removed one headphone. Cleopatra pointed at the album cover on the wall, the image from Led Zeppelin's debut album, featuring the Hindenburg disaster. "Marvin's balloon!" she exclaimed.

"That was the original," said Etty.

"Looks just like it."

Etty nodded.

"Led Zeppelin...how does it sound?" asked Cleopatra.

Etty handed Cleopatra the headphones and replied, "It's worse than jazz."

Cleopatra put on the headphones and rocked out, playing some air guitar. Etty said something to her but she couldn't hear him with Robert Plant screaming in her ears. She took off one headphone.

Etty pointed to the book in Cleopatra's hand and asked, "Why would a book be in the Museum of Pop Culture?"

"It's not from the museum. I forgot it last time I was here."

"Washington. Of course. It all makes sense now."

Cleopatra held up the book. "Sherlock Holmes. *A Scandal in Bohemia.*"

A crash was heard, then another crash, and another. Etty and Cleopatra ran to the noise and saw Khorndahgh rampaging through the ruined museum, moshing around with headphones on. Destroying exhibit after exhibit, Khorndahgh shouted, "Are you speaking to me? Are you speaking to me? No way, juvenile delinquent!" Khorndahgh continued moshing around, playing an air guitar solo as he smashed up the museum.

Steering clear of the inspired barbarian,

Cleopatra and Etty explored more of the ruined museum, soaking up the history while waiting for Khorndahgh to get the unchecked aggression out of his system. Cleopatra spotted an exhibit for the Beatles' "Sgt. Pepper's Lonely Hearts Club Band." She looked at the mural of the album cover and said, "Look at all the flowers. Pixie would've loved this one."

Etty agreed, but it didn't mean he had to like it as well. "Sergeant Pepper's Lonely Hearts Club Band...Beatles. What a stupid album title. Beatles? Beatles what? How many songs can you write about bugs?"

Cleopatra suggested, "Maybe they ran out of flowers when they got to the album title."

Etty stared at the album cover for a while, lost in the flowers and cardboard people, until he noticed that Cleopatra was gone. He soon found her in the video game wing of the museum, looking at an old video game cartridge in a glass display case.

Etty walked up and read the display plaque,

"Hall of Shame Baseball…" The cartridge in the display case was for the old 16 bit Smartyvision game console, and featured Harry Colliflower, the worst baseball player in Major League history, on the cover. This bored Etty, and he looked around for something more interesting. He found some blacklight posters, which glowed with trippy colors as he drew near, illuminated by the purplish blacklight in his brain crystals.

Hearing the sound of breaking glass, Etty turned back to see the Hall of Shame Baseball display case broken. The Hall of Shame Baseball video game cartridge was missing, as was Cleopatra. The gorilla shook his head and went off to find her.

Chapter 9: The Cosmo Dome

After their adventures in the Museum of Pop Culture, Cleopatra, Etty, and Khorndahgh zoomed through the sky towards Willie World in the 300 SL Roadster. On the way, Etty explained his plan, "We land outside the park, sneak in, steal some costumes, get a park map, and then form a snatch-and-grab plan to rescue–"

"We don't have time for all that," said Cleopatra. "We should fly in fast and low and pluck her off a ride or something."

Khorndahgh had his own concerns about the mission. He butted in from the trunk, poking his head around the back hood, "Promise you won't ride any roller coasters without me."

Etty ignored the barbarian and responded to Cleopatra, "*I* make the plan! I'm the smartest. We do it my way."

"Your plans failed twice already. We do it my way this time," said Cleopatra.

Khorndahgh was insistent, "Promise…"

Etty dispensed with the barbarian, "We promise," before continuing with Cleopatra, "My plans didn't fail. Khorndahgh screwed them up."

"She's my sister."

"I won the battle of wits," declared Etty, inspired by this very first usage of the triumph.

"It wasn't a battle of wits, it was a battle of intellect. I would slay you in a battle of wits," said Cleopatra.

"It was a battle of wits. All three and a half points you gained were by wits, not intellect."

"What about you? Can't win a battle of wits without being witty."

But, as it turns out, Etty did use wits. "Cleopatra, I don't know how zero-point energy works."

Cleopatra was stunned. "But you explained it all."

"It was a guess. I knew you didn't know the

answer either. I could have said anything."

"It was how you said it." Cleopatra was depressed, having been defeated in a battle of wits by a monkey. "I feel like Sherlock Holmes."

"Does that make me Professor Moriarty?" asked Etty, referring to Sherlock Holmes' arch-nemesis known for outwitting Sir Arthur Conan Doyle's famous fictional detective.

"Irene Adler."

"You should have asked me movie trivia."

"I thought I did."

"Anyway, it was a battle of wits, and you lost," said Etty, getting back to the point.

The sound of a bubble gum bubble popping was heard. The supercar's systems flashed on and off as smoke spewed from the tailpipe and the 300 SL began an obstreperous descent into Willie World.

"What happened?" asked Cleopatra.

"Marvin!" cried Etty. "He must have built some kind of disruption shield around the park. You flew too close, like Icarus."

"More like the Hoth system. Hang on!" Cleopatra did her best to control the descent. The 300 SL crashed through the roof of the Willie World Cosmo Dome, the smoke from the supercar trailing away and out of the hole in the enormous structure.

Seeing the Mercedes-Benz crash into the Cosmo Dome, the steampunk Nazibots at Fairy Tale Castle took their orders from Hitlerbot. The robot dictator yelled a bunch of nonsense while waving its finger as sweat flew from its overly-animated head, "Warum hat das Huhn die Straße überquert? Weil du es nicht verdammte noch gekocht hast! Du hast so viel Ingwer reingetan, das ist ein Weasley!"

A Zug of Nazibots stampeded away to investigate the crash site. By Hitlerbot's order, a second Zug of Nazibots was sent to deal with Marvin and Pixie, who were by now headed to the Circus Train. Future historians will, no doubt, debate the strategy of Hitlerbot's two-front war.

Marvin and Pixie made it safely to the Circus Train thanks to a villainous cast of Actorbots in character costumes, who fought off the pursuing steampunk Nazibots. Unlike real actors, the Actorbots laid down their robot lives to protect their fans. Some were chainsawed, some flamed, others blasted to termination by the Nazibots with steampunk blunderbusses, but they delayed the Nazibots long enough for Marvin and Pixie to enjoy the train ride without interruption.

Back at the Cosmo Dome, Cleopatra awoke to the gentle patting of her face by a big gorilla paw.

"Are you OK?" asked Etty.

"What?" Cleopatra was still in a daze after the crash. "Where are we?"

"In the gift shop," responded the ape. "You somehow managed to weave your way past all of the twisting coaster tracks. That was exceptional driving."

"Why are we in the gift shop?"

Etty pointed to a large hole in the wall. You skidded through the wall on the Cosmo Dome.

We were all thrown out."

"Khorndahgh–"

"He's fine. He went to scout. Can you move?"

"I think so." After Cleopatra was helped to her feet by Etty, she stood in her Union Jack dress, wringing her wrists. Seeing an injury to her hand, she lamented, "I broke a nail."

Etty was impatient. "Let's go."

Before they could leave, steampunk Nazibots wielding chainsaw-swords and chainsaw-axes stormed into the gift shop. Etty and Cleopatra ran through the hole in the wall, back into the Cosmo Dome, and boarded a rocket ship coaster car to escape the Nazibots. The Nazibots boarded the next coaster space rocket and gave chase. However, because the coaster cars all moved at the same speed, the Nazibots were unable to catch up to them.

Etty and Cleopatra ascended into 'outer space,' looking back to see the Nazibots behind, futilely waving their chainsaw weapons in the air. "Your hat," said Cleopatra, as they got to the top of the coaster track.

The gorilla took off the white cowboy hat and put it into his lap just before they zoomed down the first hill and sped through the Milky Way. Etty's crystals flashed with yellow light as he screamed in terror. The ape hung onto the coaster car for dear life, dizzied and sick.

Cleopatra screamed with delight, "Wooooooooooo!" and laughed as the coaster rocket car sped through the stars. She was enjoying the ride immensely and put her hands up in the air, showing her bravery.

Etty quickly forced them down. "Don't do that!" ordered the terrified gorilla.

Descending towards the end of the coaster, Cleopatra laughed again and shouted, "Woo Woo Wooooooooooo!" While passing Saturn, they could see more Nazibots awaiting them at the end of the ride. "Whatta we do?" asked Cleopatra.

"We should jump off," suggested Etty, though he had no intention of doing so, and still clung tightly to the coaster car for safety.

Cleopatra looked around, unsure, and braced herself as they passed behind Jupiter and lost sight of the Nazibots at the bottom. When the 'rocket ship' finally 'landed' into the launch bay they found a pile of Nazibot corpses, Khorndahgh standing atop them.

"You went on the roller coaster without me?" said the barbarian, disappointed. He pointed his finger at Etty. "You promised!"

"We had to escape the robots," explained Etty. "And it wasn't fun, anyway."

"It *was* fun," said Cleopatra.

Khorndahgh leaped over them and jumped from the coaster track onto the trailing Nazibots' rocket car. The energy sword called forth from the barbarian's bracers made quick work of the startled Nazibots. Khorndahgh turned back to Etty after dispatching the fascist robots. "If you're not gonna wear it…"

"I'm wearing it." Etty put the cowboy hat back on and explained, "We were flying through space, which is a vacuum so it shouldn't matter, but it wasn't really outer space, it was a dome filled with air, which causes drag, so…"

"O…K," replied Khorndahgh. Such a lengthy, rambling explanation could not be wrong.

Cleopatra asked the barbarian, "Did you find Pixie?"

"Didn't see Faerie. Found some cars."

"There aren't any cars in Willie World," said Etty.

"Come see," said Khorndahgh.

Chapter 10: Trains

Marvin and Pixie were enjoying a pleasant ride on the slow-moving Circus Train. The Actorbots had laid down their robot lives to allow the pair to enjoy this nice respite from the murderous attacks of the steampunk Nazibots.

Pixie stood in a circus cage car, holding the bars and looking out. "I'm your prisoner," she said, giggling. With the flash of her hands, she used her faerie magic to modify her ballerina tutu into a dazzling circus trapeze artist outfit.

Marvin saw only lost potential. "You aren't very good at using your powers, are you?"

Pixie looked down, sad.

"It's OK. Once I figure out the science behind it, I'll be using it to do great things." Marvin spied Cartoon City approaching. "Do you like cartoons?" he asked. Pixie didn't know what cartoons were, but she did like cute animals, which were often depicted in cartoons.

Passing by Cartoon City, they could see a furious melee going on between the steampunk Nazibots and Marvin's Actorbots wearing animal cartoon character outfits. Deranged Duck and his deranged family of ducks were hammering and sickling the Nazibots, but the fascist robots were getting the better of the ducks, slicing them up with chainsaw weapons. Duck feathers went flying everywhere as the Actorbots were cut down.

The Silly Squirrels fared no better, but Robbie Rabbit was doing some real damage before a steampunk flamethrower set the cartoon robot alight. Robbie ran around on fire, in a crazy circle, finally brought down by a flurry of steampunk crossbow bolts.

Marvin and Pixie watched on from the safety of the circus train. Marvin suggested, "Let's not visit Cartoon City."

Back at the Cosmo Dome, Khorndahgh led

Cleopatra and Etty out and to the cars he had found, which turned out to be a traffic jam of little convertible theme park cars on a track. It was, of course, the Automania ride at Willie World.

"That's a lot of cars," said Cleopatra.

Seeing Nazibots charging towards them, they each hopped in a car and drove away...very slowly.

Etty was in a yellow car next to Khorndahgh's car, which was red. "We're only going about five kilometers per hour," said the ape to the barbarian.

"Is that fast?" asked Khorndahgh.

"No," answered Etty. "We're not going to outrun them in these cars."

"The Unirail!" cried Cleopatra, who was in a blue car behind them. She pointed ahead to where the Unirail track crossed over the Automania ride. A Unirail train was approaching on the track above.

"How do we get up there?" asked Etty, looking

back to see the Nazibots gaining on them, running faster than the little cars.

Cleopatra enlisted the barbarian to help, "Khorndahgh, can you—"

"No!" warned Etty, but it was too late.

Khorndahgh hopped out of his red car and tore it from the track. He tossed it up at the Unirail train, smashing it through the front window and crushing the Uniraildriverbot inside. After the car toss, Khorndahgh snatched the cowboy hat from Etty's head and placed it on his own, then grabbed the gorilla and lifted him out of his car.

"What are you doing?!" shouted Etty, his crystals flashing yellow.

With a loud cry and Herculean spin-toss, Khorndahgh threw Etty up into the Unirail train. The gorilla landed next to the red car that had smashed through the window. Khorndahgh pulled a startled Cleopatra out of her blue car just as the Nazibots were closing in. He carried her to a Unirail support column and began climbing the ladder rungs one-handed, the other hanging onto Cleopatra. He made it up just in time to catch the Unirail train, jumping inside next to Etty and the red car. He placed the cowboy hat back on Etty's head, then set Cleopatra down in the gorilla's lap, surprising them both.

Cleopatra recovered quicker than Etty. She grabbed hold of the controls and said, "I'll drive." It was easy to drive the Unirail train, as they were on a Unirail track, sending them along toward a group of steampunk Nazibots lined up on the track ahead. Cleopatra upped the speed to maximum.

Khorndahgh stood in the front of the Unirail train and used his energy bracers to call forth a long energy lance, which he used to impale the Nazibots, piling them up on the lance like meat on a skewer. The barbarian swept the lance outward and deactivated it, dropping the skewered Nazibots. The fascist robots fell screaming and exploded on the ground with puffs of green gas.

Back on the Willie World Circus Train, Marvin and Pixie were going from car to car, heading to the front of the train. They passed through a wooded area and saw Tomorrow World through the trees. "More like Yesterdayland," said Marvin, as the site was even more hopelessly outdated than when the park was in its heyday.

The Circus Train passed the Automania ride and went under the Unirail track. The Unirail train passed over and behind the Circus Train, giving Khorndahgh and company an excellent opportunity to board the train. Carrying both gorilla and girl, the barbarian leaped down and crashed through the roof of the caboose. After recovering from the drop, they ran from the back of the train towards the steam engine. Pixie, now with Marvin on the steam engine, saw them and shouted, "Cleo!"

Marvin turned back to see Khorndahgh and company getting closer. "Barbarians!" He moved to the back of the engine and tried to decouple the train from the engine car, but was having trouble.

Khorndahgh, Etty, and Cleopatra dashed through the Circus Train cars, trying to get to Pixie before Marvin could decouple the cars. Marvin pulled out his laser pointer and tried to cut the coupler, but the laser was too weak. Having failed with the laser pointer, he extracted a glass orb filled with concentrated acid from his utility belt and dropped it in between the train cars. Smoke rose from the coupler as the acid began disintegrating the metal parts.

Before Khorndahgh and company could reach the engine, the coupler broke, and the engine car chugged away from the rest of the train. Marvin pushed the Engineerbot aside and ramped up the acceleration lever, causing the steam engine to race down the track at full speed.

Khorndahgh leaped onto the train track and began chasing the engine car. Cleopatra was about to do the same, but Etty held her back.

Cleopatra yelled, "What are you doing?!"

"Stopping you from killing yourself," answered the ape.

"We gotta save Pixie!"

"We will. I have Marvin's flight harness."

"What? Where?"

As the train cars rolled slower and slower, Etty pointed to the Cosmo Dome, now in sight again. "In the Mercedes."

"Why didn't you tell me?"

"I tried, but you wouldn't shut up. Then we got into an argument."

"I don't remember any arguments," said Cleopatra, being diplomatic.

"You don't?"

"There were some intellectual discussions."

"It takes at least two intellectuals to have an intellectual discussion."

Cleopatra conceded, "No wonder I won all those arguments."

Etty's hat-hole glowed with red light. "Let's went!"

Cleopatra and Etty hopped off the now slow-moving engineless train and headed for the Cosmo Dome gift shop.

Khorndahgh kept running down the tracks, chasing the steam engine. Marvin was alarmed to see the barbarian catching up to them. Pixie smiled and waved to Khorndahgh as the steam engine passed by the park's front entrance, headed towards a huge stucco step pyramid in a jungle of post-apocalyptic foliage.

The fake pyramid housed the Alabama Smith Tomb Robber Adventure Ride. Marvin was excited. "Tomb Robber. Gotta go on that one." He took Pixie's hand and started to jump off the fast-moving train, but stopped and asked the faerie magician, "Can you use your powers to call up an inflatable raft?"

"A what?"

"It's like a balloon, but on the ground. Something I can jump into and ride down the hill."

Pixie nodded and waved her hands in the air,

conjuring up a large inflatable kid's bounce castle filled with plastic balls. The inflatable castle hovered next to the steam engine like a theme park ride waiting for passengers.

Marvin grabbed Pixie and jumped into the inflatable castle. The castle dropped to the ground and slid down the hill, Marvin and Pixie screaming all the way. The plastic balls went flying out of the castle as Marvin and Pixie bounced around inside, sliding dangerously past trees on the hill.

The inflatable castle hit a log at the bottom of the hill, sending Marvin and Pixie somersaulting out onto the ground, right at the entrance to the Alabama Smith Tomb Robber Adventure Ride. Marvin got to his feet, with Pixie's help, then took her hand and pulled her into the stucco pyramid. Once inside, Marvin and Pixie boarded a theme park cart made to look like a military truck, and off they went.

The Tomb Robber ride was a complete terror for Pixie, who screamed and covered her eyes, despite the fact that most of the steampunk Nazi automatons had exited the ride after being given robot life by the Hat Man.

Marvin held Pixie protectively and narrated the ride, pretending to be scared. "Oh, no! Lava pit! We're going to fall in!"

Pixie opened her eyes just long enough to see the lava pit. She screamed and covered her eyes again.

They didn't fall into the lava pit, as they were on a theme park ride that went along a track. Feigning relief, Marvin exclaimed, "Oh! Just missed it. That was lucky."

The truck slowed, and scary music began playing. Pixie trembled. Marvin held her tight, but did not let up on the narration, "What is that? A Tyrannosaurus rex?! Why did it have to be dinosaurs? Ah! Oh, no! Look out! It's going to eat us!" The theme park truck accelerated past the animatronic T-rex, which narrowly missed them with its huge jaws as the truck sped by. Marvin continued, "Whew! Just missed us. I thought we were dead." Pixie added crying to her trembling.

Very real danger would soon reveal itself. The truck drove past a large model of an ancient temple surrounded by a moat. A group of steampunk Nazibots menacingly rose up from the moat water. Two more Nazibots fired steampunk crossbows from atop the temple. Marvin ducked a crossbow bolt and pulled out an electro grenade from his utility belt, tossing it into the moat to electrocute the Nazibots within. After dispensing with the moat Nazis, Marvin pulled out his shotgun and blasted the crossbow-wielding Nazibots off the temple.

More Nazibots charged from behind, chasing the truck. Seeing the Nazibots gaining on them, Marvin asked Pixie for "a little help."

Pixie flashed her hands and changed from her circus trapeze artist digs into a stylish explorer's outfit, complete with a white safari pith helmet. Marvin stared at her for a moment, waiting for the safari hat to do something, but the hat instead did nothing.

As the Nazibots closed in to attack, a huge fiberglass boulder rolled across the track. The boulder just missed the truck, but did manage to crush the pursuing Nazibots, which exploded with puffs of green gas.

Chapter 11: Boats

After escaping the stucco pyramid, Marvin began thinking about ride ratings. "That was my favorite ride so far." He turned to Pixie, "What about you?"

Pixie was glad to be a safe distance away from the Tomb Robber ride. "I liked the coffee cups, the elephants, the train, the story town, the–"

"OK, I get it. Nothing scary." Marvin turned to see the Mighty Mo fake river ahead, where a steam-powered river boat with a giant red paddle wheel was permanently docked. "Not scary," said Marvin. He took Pixie's hand and dragged her to the river boat.

Back at the Cosmo Dome gift shop, Cleopatra and Etty lifted the bent trunk hood on the smashed supercar to find the zero-point energy flight harness within. Etty explained, "The warp bubble forms inside this casing on the back. How did he get the casing to move with the warp bubble? It's ingenious."

"Does it even work?" asked Cleopatra.

"Only one way to find out," replied the ape. Etty pulled the heavy harness out of the trunk and tried to put it on. He turned around in circles in the attempt before Cleopatra hoisted it upon his shoulders. It fit the four-hundred pound gorilla fairly well, the device having been originally fitted for Marvin, who was himself a heavyset primate. Cleopatra found a pull cord and after a few pulls, like starting a gas-powered lawn mower, managed to start up the device.

After Etty argued with Cleopatra for a while about how to operate the flight harness, then crashing around the gift shop while practicing, the gorilla carried the girl back into the Cosmo Dome and up through the hole in the roof. Etty struggled to control the machine as they awkwardly flew off to find Pixie, zigging and zagging their way through the air.

By this time Marvin and Pixie were on the Willie World Riverboat. Pixie was now costumed in a purple nineteenth century dress of high fashion and carried with her a purple parasol to shield her from the huge blazing sun descending to the horizon. They were on the top deck near the gigantic red paddle wheel, which was paddling despite the fact the boat was permanently docked. Looking over the paddle wheel, they saw a horde of steampunk Nazibots on land charging towards the river.

Marvin and Pixie watched on as a line of Actorbots dressed in fairy tale princess costumes guarded the riverbank. The princesses used their hammers and sickles to fell a few of the Nazibots, while the Nazibots used their chainsaw weapons to decapitate, delimb, and impale the princesses.

Rapunzel and her beautiful hair were cut in half at the waist. Mulan took a chainsaw-spear through the face. Sleeping Beauty was put to sleep by steampunk crossbow bolts. Briar Rose was decapitated, as was Pocahontas. Princess

Anna was run through by a chainsaw-sword. A battle-dancing Cinderella was delimbed by Nazibot chainsaw-axes as she danced around. Snow White took a direct hit from a steampunk flamethrower, turning her snow white skin coal black.

Having dealt with the princesses, the Nazibots charged towards the docked riverboat. Marvin was about to pull a gadget from his utility belt, but stopped when he saw Pixie waving her hands in the air, casting a faerie spell. Line after line of purple faerie seahorses, the size of real horses, leaped out of the river and hopped towards the Nazibots, exploding into purple glitter as the fascist robots cut them down. The Nazibots resumed their charge towards the riverboat after being delayed by the sea horses.

The delay would prove deadly for the Nazibots, as Khorndahgh was now on the scene, having run through the jungle in pursuit. The barbarian circled around like a ballet dancer, chopping down Nazibots left and right with his energy axes. Khorndahgh activated an energy shield to block a fire stream from the steampunk flamethrower, then advanced on the flames until the flamethrower stream reflected off the barbarian's energy shield, back at the flame-throwing Nazi robot, melting it. After dispensing with the Nazibots, Khorndahgh ran to the riverboat's docking bridge.

Marvin extracted a sticky bomb from his utility belt and threw it at the barbarian. The sticky bomb exploded into a glue-like substance, holding Khorndahgh in place. As Khorndahgh struggled to escape the sticky mess, Marvin pulled his magnetron laser pointer from his pocket and said, "I'll burn his eyes out."

"Etty!" shouted Pixie.

"Eddie?" said Marvin. He turned to see Etty flying his zero-point energy supercharged mercury centrifuge powered flight harness, carrying Cleopatra. "Eighty!" Marvin pocketed the laser pointer and produced a stick from an orb on his utility belt. The stick expanded, then bloomed into a festival of balloons, each shaped like the head of Steamboat Willie.

Pixie turned back to see Khorndahgh still struggling to break free from the sticky bomb. She gesticulated, calling a river wave in the shape of a blue whale to wash over Khorndahgh and dissolve the sticky strands binding him. Now free, Khorndahgh leaped up onto the riverboat and began climbing to the top. Seeing the barbarian closing in, Marvin grabbed Pixie and tugged on the balloons, which bore them swiftly away, over an island and to a pirate ship.

Etty and Cleopatra gave chase, zig-zagging their way to the pirate ship. Khorndahgh dove off the riverboat and swiftly swam in pursuit.

Once aboard the pirate ship, Marvin let go of the balloons, which floated up and away. From his utility belt he extracted a small rectangular metal box with a big red button. The box was labeled, 'PIRATES'. Marvin pushed the big red button and Piratebots came running up onto the deck, waving their cutlasses in the air.

"Whatta we do?" asked Etty.

"Drop me on Marvin," said Cleopatra.

"Are you crazy?!"

"Do it!"

Etty zigged, zagged, overshot Marvin, then reversed until he was directly over the target.

By now Marvin was ready with his shotgun. He set his gunsights on Etty, but before he could pull the trigger a glint of sunlight reflected off of Cleopatra's gold cross necklace, blinding him. He covered his eyes with his left hand, causing the one-handed blind shotgun blast to miss wildly. Cleopatra landed on top of Marvin and he fell to the deck, the shotgun dropping from his hand.

Etty smashed a couple of Piratebots as he landed on the deck of the ship. The gorilla snatched up one of the fallen Piratebot's cutlasses and slashed at the air to get a feel for the blade.

Cleopatra sat up, straddling her legs over Marvin, and socked him right in his fat nose. Marvin slapped her off and held his nose, blood streaming from it. "You...you broke my nose!" he screamed as he rolled onto his stomach, preparing to begin the standing up procedure. Blood poured from his broken nose, staining the ship's deck. Cleopatra jumped at Marvin but was knocked to the ground by a Cabinboybot's belaying pin. The Cabinboybot was quickly felled by Etty's cutlass.

Marvin got to his feet and picked up his electroball shotgun. He pointed to the flight harness Etty was wearing and said, "That belongs to me."

"Who's smart enough to understand z-point energy now?" mocked Etty, before swooping into the air. Marvin pumped and fired his shotgun, but Etty zigged and zagged, dodging the electroballs.

Marvin shot and missed a few more times before Etty was able to sever some sail lines with his cutlass, causing the sail to fall upon Marvin and his Piratebot guards. The huge sail also fell upon Pixie as she raced to her sister, and she fell to the deck.

Etty laughed and began to descend, intent on rescuing Pixie. As he did so, a flintlock pistol shot whizzed by him, hitting a line on the flight harness causing an air blast to shoot out. The flight harness spun around in circles as it fell from the sky and crashed onto the poop deck at the ship's stern, smashing the ship's wheel to pieces.

The flintlock pistol was fired by none other than CaptainHookbot. The robot pirate captain put the flintlock pistol in its belt and drew its cutlass, pointing the pirate sword at Etty. Piratebots charged at the gorilla, who quickly removed the damaged flight harness and fought them off with his cutlass.

One of the Piratebots came up behind Etty, but was cut down at the knees by Cleopatra below, wielding a cutlass from the ship's ladder. Etty pulled her up to the poop deck and they stood back to back, fighting off the mechanical pirates, cutlass on cutlass.

As CaptainHookbot advanced on the pair, its ridiculous feathered pirate hat was snatched off its head by Khorndahgh swinging by on a rope. The barbarian had, by now, boarded the ship after his record-breaking swim. Khorndahgh leaped down to Cleopatra and Etty, put on the ridiculous pirate hat, and said to the robot pirate captain, "I'm the captain now."

CaptainHookbot swung its cutlass at Khorndahgh, but the pirate sword was sliced in half by the barbarian's British navy energy cutlass, brought forth from his energy bracers. Khorndahgh called up an energy machete into his other hand and attacked, but CaptainHookbot caught it with its negative energy glassteel hook and twisted, disabling the energy weapon. Khorndahgh's energy cutlass met the same fate, leaving the barbarian weaponless.

Khorndhagh ducked a couple of hook attacks, trying to call more weapons from his energy bracers, but got only sparks. The weaponless barbarian evaded another hook slash by jumping to a Jacob's ladder that rose up to the top of the main mast. Cleopatra tossed a Piratebot cutlass to Khorndahgh, who clenched it in his teeth and climbed up the rope ladder.

CaptainHookbot leaped down to the main deck then chased the barbarian upward, using its hook to climb the main mast. They both swung up to the top yard and battled cutlass on hook, back and forth upon the yard.

Below, Etty and Cleopatra continued fighting the Piratebots, but there were too many of them, and they soon found themselves surrounded. Just as all seemed lost, faerie magic dolphins leaped out of the water and over the deck, summoned by Pixie who had escaped the fallen sail.

The dolphins threw the glass bottles from their noses onto the pirate ship. The faerie magic glass bottles exploded into glassy glitter on the ship's deck, then reconstituted into giant glass bottles encasing the Piratebots that were surrounding Etty and Cleopatra. The Piratebots cursed at the heroes from their glass prisons.

Etty and Cleopatra jumped down to the main deck and finished off the rest of the Piratebots with their cutlasses. The Piratebots defeated, Pixie ran to her sister and they hugged, reunited once again.

Above, Khorndhagh and CaptainHookbot continued their duel. The barbarian leaped over a hook slash and swung on the crow's nest, kicking CaptainHookbot off the main yard and into the jaws of a large mechanical theme park shark waiting in the river. The shark slowly pulled the screaming robot pirate captain underwater.

But it wasn't over. A small-scale Nazi U-boat submarine carrying steampunk Nazibots surfaced and powered its way towards the pirate ship. Cleopatra alerted Pixie, "Stop that sub, sis!"

Pixie waved her hands in the air, conjuring up an iceberg, which swiftly floated toward the U-boat. Before the iceberg could strike, the U-boat let loose a torpedo at the pirate ship. The submarine turned to avoid the faerie iceberg, but the iceberg turned as well and collided with the U-boat, exploding into icy glitter and freezing the fascist submarine, which broke in half. The U-boat and its Nazibot crew sank to the bottom of the Mighty Mo.

The U-boat's torpedo slammed into the pirate ship's bow. The ship's hull exploded into wood shards. The jolt of the collision threw Cleopatra into the main mast, knocking her unconscious. Pixie fell to the deck. The giant glass faerie bottles imprisoning the Piratebots tipped over and rolled around, some falling into the river. Above, Khorndhagh was thrown to the fore top sail, which he stabbed with his cutlass. The barbarian shouted, "Hurra!" as he heroically slid down the sail, the cutlass slicing through it as he descended. Etty was thrown into the water by the blast, which was a problem because the gorilla had no idea how to swim.

Recovering from the torpedo strike, Pixie turned to see her sister being carried away by Marvin, who, after escaping the sail, had activated large mechanical angel wings from his baby seal fur mantle. Blood continued to pour from Marvin's broken nose, staining his fancy white prince suit and leaving streaks of red across the angel wings and baby seal fur mantle.

The pirate ship was sinking fast. Pixie looked for a life boat, but there were none. Hearing Etty crying for help, she jumped into the water next to him before remembering that she couldn't swim either. She clung to Etty, dragging them both down.

With his archenemies at the bottom of the Mighty Mo, Marvin flew to Sploosh Mountain and deposited the unconscious Cleopatra into a large theme park canoe in the fabricated waterway. He retracted his bloodied angel wings and landed in the canoe behind Cleopatra. After tearing off part of his princely white cape, Marvin shoved the torn off rags up his nose to stop the bleeding, causing him to twice cry out in pain.

As the canoe climbed up the conveyor belt to the top, Marvin pulled out his pump action electroball shotgun, ready for any waiting Nazibots. The canoe got to the top and gently floated along the artificial mountain waterway with no robots in sight.

The canoe floated past animatronic animals wearing funny hats, singing a silly song. Marvin was displeased, and complained, "What the hell is this? Animals don't wear hats!" before blasting a few with his shotgun. The rest of the ride was similarly weird, with strange characters, weird lighting, and giant mushrooms. Marvin commented, "This ride was made by people on drugs. For people on drugs."

Marvin didn't like this ride, no matter what Cleopatra said, which was nothing. Neither did he like the big splooshdown at the end, which got him all wet and woke up Cleopatra. Cleopatra immediately put her hands around Marvin's throat and began choking him. The bloody snot rags shot from Marvin's broken nose, and blood began pouring down Cleopatra's arms.

It was a particularly bad time for the conflict

due to the Nazibots charging from the ride's exit into the boarding station. Marvin blasted one of the Nazibots with his shotgun but was unable to reload while being strangled by Cleopatra. He swatted away a Nazibot's chainsaw-axe attack with the shotgun, then knocked the robot's head off on the return backhand swipe.

Gasping for air, Marvin pulled out the magnetron laser pointer with his left hand and struggled to yell, "Na...zi...bots! Na...zi...bots!" Cleopatra was undeterred and continued to strangle Marvin, who tried to use his laser pointer on the fascist robots, but the laser pointer's batteries were drained.

Another Nazibot came down on Marvin with its chainsaw-sword, but Marvin parried it with his shotgun. He screamed like a girl as the chainsaw-sword began sawing through the shotgun. The sawed shotgun exploded into an electrical cloud that felled the Nazibot, and left Marvin's right arm completely numb. He dropped the spent laser pointer from his left hand and gasped for air as Cleopatra's grip tightened around his throat.

Marvin was desperate. He pulled off his utility belt with his left hand and swung it around above his head. Fire grenades, electro grenades, and acid grenades flew out of the utility belt, along with a rubber chicken, a velvet pouch full of role-playing game dice, and a deck of cards. The advancing Nazibots were burned, electrocuted, and melted by the exploding grenades, while another was slapped across the face by the rubber chicken, which demoralized the robot to the point that it moped away in retreat.

The Nazibots defeated, Marvin now turned his attention to his would-be murderer. He put his left palm on Cleopatra's face and pushed, but Cleopatra would not let go, and Marvin grew weak. He just managed to meekly say, "bar...bear...ee...uns..."

Khorndahgh had arrived on the scene with Etty and Pixie. Our heroes did not drown, of course. Khorndahgh had survived the sinking pirate ship by diving into the river, jumping the large mechanical theme park shark in the process. The barbarian was an excellent swimmer, and managed to rescue both the girl and gorilla from the river bottom. And now, here they were, having caught up to Marvin.

Marvin activated his angel wings and flew out of the canoe. Cleopatra lost her grip and fell. Khorndahgh was there to catch her, but in doing so was not able to stop Marvin from snatching up Pixie, who was now wearing a stylish Native American Pocahontas outfit. As Marvin ascended, Etty managed to grab his leg. The gorilla was pulled into the air with Marvin and Pixie, the blood from Marvin's broken nose splattering Etty's fur.

Marvin flew towards Fairy Tale Castle, carrying Pixie and Etty. On the way there, he soared over the Willie World Haunted House and said to the ape, "Drop Dead!" before kicking Etty in the face. The gorilla lost his grip and went crashing through the haunted roof.

After dropping Etty, Marvin flew off with Pixie to Fairy Tale Castle. Khorndahgh and Cleopatra ran to the Haunted House to check on Etty.

Chapter 12: Hitlerbot

Once inside the Haunted House, Khorndahgh and Cleopatra were faced with theme park monsters. Cleopatra soon realized that the ghosts and goblins were not real, but for amusement. Khorndahgh did not. The barbarian ran around the haunted house, slaying the theme park monsters with his energy weapons, which were glitchy, but working again.

Cleopatra found Etty in the dining room, fighting off ghosts. The gorilla's cowboy hat was nowhere to be seen, and his crystals glowed with yellow light. She shouted, "Etty! They're not real!"

Etty stopped fighting the ghosts, his brain crystals aglow with pink light. "I know that."

"Didn't look like it."

"I was just dazed," insisted the ape. "Where's

Khorndahgh?"

"He's killing the fake monsters. Let's go."

"What about Khorndahgh?"

"Marvin's got nothing left. If we can clip his wings he'll be at the mercy of a four-hundred pound gorilla."

"Three-eighty."

Cleopatra respected Etty's big fat lie. "C'mon. Khorndahgh will catch up."

On their way out of the Haunted House, Etty angrily smashed a fun house mirror reflecting the image of a large, hulking, black furry monster with a red light on its head. Exiting the Haunted House, the girl and gorilla sprinted to Fairy Tale Castle.

Still carrying Pixie through the sky, Marvin neared the castle. Pixie struggled to cast a faerie spell, but Marvin held her tight with his one good arm, preventing her from using her faerie magic.

A huge Navaronian gun perched on the castle walls turned to the sky and fired a shot at the airborne invaders. Marvin didn't see the gun, and was saved only by Pixie's squirm. The Navaronian artillery projectile just missed Marvin, but did manage to blast off one of his angel wings, causing Marvin and Pixie to spiral downward and crash into the castle.

Due to the forced perspective design of the castle, making the upper tiers of the building look much bigger than they actually were, it appeared to Cleopatra and Etty that Marvin and Pixie were giants crashing through the castle's roof.

The Navaronian gun turned its sights on Cleopatra and Etty, sending a mighty artillery shot whistling towards them. Etty put his paws up, expecting the end.

"I got it!" yelled Khorndahgh, now on the scene, and wearing the white cowboy hat. He fielded the artillery shot like a center fielder hogging all the glory. The artillery projectile was only the size of a walnut due to the fact that the Navaronian gun was actually quite small, appearing large only because of the forced perspective trick.

"Fastball!" cried Khorndahgh, pitching the tiny projectile back at the Navaronian gun. The pitched projectile blasted the parapet away, causing the Navaronian gun to crash down the side of the castle, appearing smaller and smaller as it tumbled down, before thunking into the castle's moat with a small splash.

Khorndahgh put the cowboy hat on Etty's startled head and said, "Chodźmy!" then dashed away to the castle. Cleopatra followed, running past Etty, who chased after.

Crashing through the castle roof, Marvin flipped over and spiraled down, landing in the throne room and on top of Hitlerbot. Pixie landed on Marvin's big belly and bounced off onto the floor, rolling to the wall.

Hitlerbot struggled to get out from under Marvin, and was quite upset about the whole situation. The robot Führer screamed, "Du verdammter Esel!" as sweat flew from its overly-animated head.

A steampunk Schutzstaffelbot with an SS honor dagger advanced on Marvin, who slapped away the robot with his one remaining angel wing. The SS Nazibot advanced again. Marvin reached into his pocket, intending to pull out his trusty Swiss Army laser knife, but instead had in hand the key to the Mercedes. He used the angel wing to swat at the SS Nazibot again, but the Nazi robot grabbed hold of it and cut it off.

After the de-winging, the SS Nazibot slashed at Marvin, who was able to parry the German steel blade with his German steel car key. Still on his back, Marvin dueled with the SS Nazibot, dagger on car key, like a tiny sword fight.

Hitlerbot, still pinned under Marvin's rotund form, screamed more nonsense, "Dieses Soufflé ist so stark versunken, dass James Cameron einen Film darüber drehen möchte!"

Pixie struggled to her feet, using the castle wall to aid her. The now-wingless Marvin, full of adrenaline, athletically rolled off der Führer and popped up, slashing the SS Nazibot's gas mask hose with his car key, causing the fascist robot to fall to the ground and writhe around as green gas shot out of the severed hose.

Hitlerbot jumped to its feet, screaming nonsense. Three more steampunk SS Nazibots entered the throne room with Walther P38 pistols in hand, and advanced on Marvin, who stood before Pixie to protect her. "Du Esel!" screamed the Führer. The SS robots fired their pistols at Marvin and Pixie, filling the room with gunsmoke.

When Khorndahgh, Etty, and Cleopatra reached the castle's moat bridge, a Zug of steampunk Nazibots were waiting for them. Khorndhagh called up an energy sword and shield from his bracers and proceeded to tear through the Nazi robots, using his shield to block their attacks.

Etty and Cleopatra crept forward behind Khorndahgh as he sliced and diced the robots, alerting the barbarian to various Nazibot attacks. After Khorndahgh finished off the last of the

Nazibots by bashing it into the moat with his energy shield, Cleopatra and Etty looked at each other and did a high five.

But it wasn't over. The chopped up Nazibot robot remains began slowly crawling towards them. "C'mon!" shouted Etty, seeing no point in the fight.

"Wait!" Cleopatra picked up a terminated Nazibot's steampunk flamethrower and, with a devilish gleam in her eyes, let loose on the stubborn Nazibot remains. The Nazibot remnants were melted in a hellish display, the fascist machines' decapitated heads letting out foul cries as they burned.

Khorndahgh and Etty, their mouths agape, glanced at the girl, shocked by the glee with which she executed the task. "Let's went...into the castle," said Cleopatra, before dropping the flamethrower and rushing into the castle to save Pixie. Khorndhagh and Etty dashed after her.

Inside the castle, Marvin and Pixie were not dead. As it turns out, the Nazibots' Walther P38s were merely props from the Alabama Smith Tomb Robber Adventure Ride, and fired no actual bullets. But the SS Nazibots still had their daggers, which were quite real.

Pixie stood behind Marvin, using her faerie magic to conjure up a flutter of faerie butterflies the size of seahawks. The SS Nazibots swung their daggers around, slashing at the butterflies, which exploded into colorful glitter when hit.

After the steampunk SS Nazibots finished off the butterflies, they turned to Marvin and Pixie. Marvin held up his car key, determined to fight to the end, but the SS Nazibots stopped in their tracks when they saw Khorndahgh and his friends, who had just arrived.

With an energy sword in one hand, and an energy axe in the other, Khorndhagh leaped at the Schutzstaffelbots and cut them to pieces.

Hitlerbot waved its finger in the air and yelled a bunch of nonsense at the barbarian, the robot's overly-animated head throwing sweat, "Bereiten wir eine Suppe zu oder versuchen wir, einen

Dämon heraufzubeschwören?!"

Khorndahgh cut Hitlerbot in half at the waist with a spinning energy sword attack, felling the robot Führer. The barbarian turned to his friends and said with a smile, "I killed–"

"Im Moment würde ich lieber Pudelmist essen, als das in meinen Mund zu nehmen!" Hitlerbot was not quite dead yet.

Khorndahgh brought down his energy axe, decapitating der Führer, finishing the robot dictator once and for all. Khorndahgh again turned to his friends and said, "I killed–"

"Für das, was wir gleich essen werden, möge der Herr dafür sorgen, dass wir wirklich nicht erbrechen!" Hitlerbot was still not dead. The heroes watched on as the robot Führer's headless body pulled out its Walther PPK pistol and shot itself in its decapitated head, finally terminating the fascist machine.

"Hitler killed Hitler!" cried Cleopatra.

Khorndahgh frowned.

Cleopatra looked around and said, "Where's

Pixie?"

Etty added, "Where's Marvin?" Hearing a scream from Pixie coming from outside of the castle, the heroes dashed away!

Marvin was carrying Pixie over his shoulder with his one good arm, and running through Americaland, laughing all the way. Pixie tried to cast a faerie magic spell, but the jolting of being carried by Marvin caused the spell to fail, creating cute furry faerie animals with horrible genetic defects. The twisted faerie animals crawled along the streets of Americaland, leaving trails of faerie blood in their wake. They cried in a disordered, microtonal chorus, "Kill me...," before exploding one by one into bloody glitter.

Khorndahgh, Etty, and Cleopatra chased after Marvin, but soon realized why he was so jolly. A gigantic, kaiju-sized Steamboat Willie robot was tramping towards them, smashing roller coasters and other rides while laughing a bubbly, squeaky laugh. The heroes bravely charged forward, intent on rescuing Pixie, who was being placed by

Marvin into a rocket that was rising up out of the Great Americaland fountain.

Khorndahgh ran straight at SteamboatWilliebot, which tried to crush the barbarian under foot. Khorndhagh leaped and caught the front of Steamboat Willie's robotic shoe, then somersaulted on top of it. The barbarian cried, "Warsaw!" An energy war saw appeared in his hand, which he used to quickly saw through the gigantic robot's thin leg. The gargantuan Steamboat Willie robot, now footless and unbalanced, fell hard into Fairy Tale Castle, smashing the structure to rubble, and breaking the huge robot apart.

Cleopatra and Etty had, by now, caught up to Marvin, but he was already in the rocket, and about to close the door when Cleopatra yelled, "Baseball!"

Marvin was confused, but he did not immediately close the rocket door. "What?"

Cleopatra confidently said, "We challenge you to a baseball match."

Marvin corrected her, "Baseball *game.*"

Etty was worried, saying to Cleopatra, "Are you sure this is a good idea?"

Cleopatra ignored Etty and said to Marvin, "Me and my friends against you and your robots. If we win, you have to let us all go and never bother us again."

Marvin smiled, "And when I win?"

Cleopatra paused before expelling, like vomit, the words, "I'll marry you."

Etty could not contain his horror, "No!"

Marvin quickly accepted Cleopatra's terms. "Deal!"

Seeing the rocket near-ready for take-off, Cleopatra quickly added, "Pixie's on our team. Let her go."

Marvin shoved Pixie out of the rocket, which by now was rising higher out of the launch tube. Pixie screamed as she fell. Etty gasped and began to leap for the girl, but Khorndahgh, now on the scene, caught her in his arms and set her down. Marvin shouted, "I'll send a transport for you in one week."

Cleopatra countered, "One month. We need time to get our team together, and to practice."

"Two weeks," said Marvin.

"Three weeks."

"Fine," conceded Marvin, now closing the door just as the rocket ascended from the launch tube and shot towards the heavens.

Khorndhagh tackled the girls and gorilla into the fountain to save them from the rocket's fire. Once the rocket was away, they stood up, soaked in fountain water.

Khorndhagh and Etty watched the rocket ascend into the shimmering stellary night as the twin sisters hugged each other. Etty could appreciate that Cleopatra had bartered a deal that had them all together. He turned to her and said, "You don't really mean to play the baseball game, right? It was all a ruse, I presume, to get us all together."

"No," responded Cleopatra. "We play the game."

"Are you crazy? We can't win."

"We can if Marvin plays like Harry Colliflower." From her drenched Union Jack dress, Cleopatra pulled out the Hall of Shame Baseball video game cartridge she had stolen from the Pop museum and showed it to Etty.

"This isn't a video game," said the gorilla.

"It is to Marvin's robot baseball bat. I just need to get a hold of it for a minute."

"We need a plan," said Etty, his hat-hole aglow with blacklight.

"We need to get our team together first."

Khorndahgh suggested, "Umbatu, Honey..."

"Yu Tou and William," added Pixie.

"That's eight," said Etty. "We just need one more."

"Alright. Let's went!" cried Cleopatra.

The heroes leaped into action!

THE END.

Thank You
God, Family, Friends

Special Thanks
Michael Cop